twixt mas

twixt mas

an aunt enid christmas story (of sorts)

KAREN J CARLISLE

Kraken Publishing

twixtmas

An Aunt Enid Christmas story (of sorts)

 A catalogue record for this book is available from the National Library of Australia

ISBN: 978-0-6458151-2-2
Series: Carlisle, Karen J. The Aunt Enid Mysteries Book 3
Also available separately as eBook

This book is written in British English.
Printed in Australia.
Typeset in Times Roman 12pt.

Published by Kraken Publishing.
www.krakenpublishing.com

To David Brooks, who first introduced me to the Howler,
to my readers, for their patience,
and to my friends,
who stand by me on the bad days.

contents

twixtmas:

an aunt enid christmas story (of sorts)

bonus extras

chapter one

A hot wind blustered along the driveway. Small dust eddies settled on Agnes' freshly polished Wolseley in the driveway. In the back yard, bees buzzed around Enid Turner's head. She muttered, trying to settle the bees as she lifted a damp tablecloth from a bare patch in the scorched grass.

The ancient washing machine clanked and groaned intermittently in the old laundry shed, as Agnes wrestled it into submission.

The bees pirouetted and danced around Enid's head.

"Not now." She waved them away with her silver walking cane.

A loud bang shuddered the laundry walls. Smoke erupted from the door.

The bees darted back to their hive.

"Blast!" Agnes emerged from the dispersing smoke.

Another clatter of metal.

"You'll need a new one," said Agnes.

Enid sighed. Electrical appliances never fared well near Protectors. Keeping it, and her freezer, in the laundry shed provided a buffer zone. Still, she was surprised it had lasted as long as it had.

"Perhaps we should get the freezer checked," she said. "I can't let it break down. It's full of cakes for the New Year's charity stall."

The grandmother clock chimed faintly in the hall.

"Alfred will be here soon." Enid flicked the soiled tablecloth. A dust cloud enveloped her. She frowned.

"I'll be with you in a minute." Agnes wiped grease off her hands and stared back into the laundry.

Enid sniffed the air. There was a faint odour, mixed with the smell of hot oil, coming from the house. The smell of burning —

She dropped the tablecloth. "The gingerbread!"

Enid raced inside. The screen door slapped behind her. A charcoal-coloured feline padded along the hallway after her, trailing silver tinsel behind him.

Bells tinkled on the bead curtain as they entered the kitchen. Smoke licked the ceiling.

Enid snatched up a quilted oven mitt, flung open one of the oven doors, and rescued a baking tray from the belly of the old, wood-burning stove. The metal tray clattered on the bench.

The cat's fur tickled her as he wrapped around her legs.

"Not now, Mr B." Enid slumped into a kitchen chair and ignored his affections.

Jingling bells danced on the bead curtain as Agnes rushed into the kitchen. She threw open the window above the sink, and fanned the smoke outside.

Mr B took shelter under the table.

"No clean tablecloth, and now no gingerbread. What will Alfred think? It's our first Christmas dinner."

"I don't think he'll be examining the tablecloth," replied Agnes.

Enid felt her cheeks burn.

Mr B growled.

Enid patted his soft fur. He rubbed his head against her hand, circled the chair, and paraded out of the room. Tinsel sashayed and shimmered in his wake.

Another wind gust caught the lace curtains. Dust filled the room. Enid swallowed; the scorching heat had already heralded hordes of Darkness this summer, and raging bush fires the year before. What would the new year bring?

Her chair scraped along the tiles as she jumped to her feet. She emptied the coffee grounds from the percolator, strode out the front door, and sprinkled them around the hydrangeas.

Heat radiated off the concrete driveway. The air shimmered. Enid shaded her eyes and searched the bushland beyond the hawthorn hedge. It was a dangerous time of year. The barriers between connected worlds were thinning; anything could breach their protective shells. And this heat only made it easier.

It was her job to protect this world.

She pushed the grounds into the soil with her shoe as she rubbed the petals through her fingers, and clicked her tongue. They could never be too blue.

The hum of a perfectly-tuned engine purred along the road. A sleek BMW turned into the driveway. The gravel crunched.

Enid's heart leapt.

Alfred leaned out the window, tipped his hat, and smiled.

"You're early." She dusted off her hands.

Agnes joined her on the verandah and waved a tea towel in his direction.

"I thought I'd help with setting up." He reached into the back seat. "Has the tree arrived? I've got a box of decorations in the car boot."

"It was a lovely thought," said Agnes. "Sally will love it."

"We had to rearrange the furniture to fit it in." Enid retrieved the cardboard box from the boot.

"I'll put the kettle on." Agnes returned to the house.

They followed Agnes inside.

Mr B skittered along the tiles past them.

Alfred removed his hat and hung it on the hallway hat rack. Enid continued into the lounge room. Mr B was already there, curled up on Alfred's usual armchair, his tail batting the Christmas tree.

Alfred grinned and placed a box, wrapped in silvered paper and tied with curled green ribbon, on the coffee table. He scanned the decorations; old-fashioned strung popcorn and paper chains hung amongst ivy and holly. Miniature candles were clipped to the ends of the branches. "I haven't seen paper chains since I was a boy."

Enid clasped his hand. "Good memories, I hope." She leaned her silver walking stick, etched with spiral vinework, against the settee and sat down.

"Very." He sat next to her.

Mr B's eyes narrowed.

Enid eyed the box. "For me?"

"For everyone," he replied. "You'll get yours later."

Mr B launched off the armchair onto Enid's lap, circled twice and lay down. Alfred leaned back.

Enid glared at the cat. "I'm sorry."

Teacups rattled as Agnes entered the room.

"He's jealous." She placed a tray with four teacups - one full of coffee - on the table and sat on the vacated armchair opposite them. "Sally's shift is finished. She should be here soon." She lifted the teapot. "I'll be Mother, shall I?" Agnes filled two of the teacups.

Mr B sniffed Enid's cup and purred. Enid ignored him, and sipped her coffee.

Agnes eyed the present. "Well, open it."

Enid finished her coffee, slowly slipped off the ribbon, and carefully removed the wrapping paper. Inside was a flat, square box, an envelope and a brown paper parcel wrapped in plastic.

She opened the box first. The rich smell of fruit, brown sugar, and brandy enveloped her. Agnes licked her lips.

Alfred smiled.

"I soaked the fruit for three weeks. And this…" Alfred pulled out the envelope and handed it to Enid. "This is for you," he said.

Enid opened the envelope. Inside was a page of yellowing paper, with fine handwriting in faded ink.

"My grandmother's recipe," he said. "I haven't any sisters, so it passed to me. I wanted to pass it onto someone special."

"But your son?" asked Enid.

Alfred chuckled. "He's not a fan of fruitcake. They have a barbecue for Christmas. All the sausages and chops you can eat."

Enid slipped the recipe back into the envelope and hugged him.

Mr B's fur prickled. His tail twitched as he stared at them with slitted eyes.

"Who's this one for?" Agnes retrieved the plastic-wrapped parcel.

"A present for Mr B," said Alfred.

The cat's tail froze. He sniffed the parcel.

"Best put it in the fridge," said Alfred. "Roo meat. Don't let him scoff it all at once, mind. My old tabby was addicted to it."

Agnes winked at Enid. "I'll fetch the bowl."

Mr B licked his paws, stepped off Enid's lap, and trotted into the hallway. The bells on the kitchen door's bead curtain tinkled. He yowled for Agnes to hurry up.

"I should help Agnes in the kitchen, if we're going to get the baking done before Sally arrives." Enid rested her hand on Alfred's arm. "Well played."

Alfred smiled and sipped his tea.

chapter two

The car radio crackled. Sally twiddled a knob on the dash. Music blared, then faded into an intermittent hiss. She thumped the dash, and groaned. The plastic beads of the friendship bracelet, on her left wrist, caught on the indicator lever. They clacked as she unhooked them.

The pale blue hatchback turned into her Great Aunt Enid's driveway. Tinsel glinted on the rearview mirror; a kaleidoscope of sparkling red, green, and gold tracked across the roof. The car shuddered to a stop behind Alfred's Beamer.

Hot air blasted through the open window. The aircon had long gone, thanks to Aether-interference. Sally tapped her gloved fingers on the steering wheel and huffed; no wonder the aircon in her aunt's house was always on the fritz.

She rolled her shoulders; it'd been a long shift, full of drunks, broken bones, and accident-prone patients.

A bee hovered outside the window, dipping and rising with each wind current.

Sally cranked the window shut, retrieved a brightly-wrapped present and a large duffel bag from the back seat, then opened the car door. A hint of smoke and oil lingered in the air. She scanned the back yard. The washing line was empty and the laundry shed, behind Agnes and Alfred's cars, was shut tight. A flank of mismatched garden gnomes had already formed behind her. Red - her aunt's favourite - stood point.

She hesitated. Though her aunt's garden gnome army had proven useful last summer, they still unnerved her. She sucked in a deep breath, snatched up a length of tinsel from the mirror, and slammed the car door shut with her foot. It creaked ominously.

Her muscles flinched.

"They're on our side," she whispered. "Where's my—" She turned on her heel to avoid the nearest garden gnome. "Where's my aunt?" she asked the bee.

The bee buzzed and flew towards the house.

It'd been agreed - at least between Aunt Enid and Aunt Agnes - she'd stay with her Great Aunt over the Christmas break. Both aunts had been adamant about it. All weather predictions were for another hot summer. This was a bad omen apparently, and the Protectors needed to regroup. Exactly what that meant, and why, Sally wasn't sure, but the aunts had promised they'd explain when she arrived.

Another scorching wind rushed up from the gully, whipping her hair across her face. She inhaled slowly, drinking in the crisp scent of tea tree and eucalyptus. The wind whistled along the verandah and circled back, ripping through the long grass to reveal the pointed ceramic caps of more garden gnomes dotted throughout the front yard. Waiting…

Sally swallowed. *They're on our side*. Heat pricked her fingers as her magic rallied to her defense. She avoided their black pupil-less eyes and concentrated on their leader, Red. He'd protected her when it mattered.

The wind changed direction, bringing with it the heady perfume of her aunt's hawthorn perimeter hedge. Her aunt had constructed an enchantment to keep it in flower, providing limited protection all year round. She allowed her muscles to relax. Her fingers cooled.

Another deep breath. It was a contradictory aroma. To her, it smelled of the reassuring almond-like spiciness of vanilla, and aniseed; to others, the sickly stench of death.

The bee returned, buzzing insistently.

"Merry Christmas, Red." She patted his head hesitantly, wound the green tinsel around the garden gnome's red cap as she dragged the duffel bag over her shoulder, and picked her way through the grass towards the house.

An old shovel leaned against the wall by the front door. The aroma of coffee grounds and chicken manure originated from beneath the hydrangeas on either side of the verandah step. Their blooms were a deep, reassuring blue.

A lace curtain fluttered through the open kitchen window to her right. The smell of smoke was stronger now. Pots clattered inside. Aunt Enid laughed. A chuckle followed; the deep, gentle voice of their new friend Alfred.

Sally smiled and knocked on the screen door.

"Door's open." Aunt Enid's voice wafted through the window.

Sally balanced her aunt's present on her hip and pushed open the door.

The smell of fresh pine rolled over her. Old Christmas

carols played in the lounge room.

A blur of charcoal ran between her legs and skidded on the floor tiles into the kitchen.

"Is that you, Sally?" Another voice, from the lounge room.

Sally dropped her keys in the bowl on the hall table. "Yes, Aunt Agnes."

Sally manoeuvred around an armchair, pushed close to the lounge room doorway. The settee was also out of place, dragged under the window to accommodate a three-metre pine tree wedged in the corner, opposite the fireplace. Its branches dripped with silver tinsel, baubles, and miniature candles clipped to branch tips. A glitter-covered star hung from its bent tip, pushed hard against the ceiling. The branches shivered, shedding needles onto the carpet.

A record rotated on the dusty stereogram in the far corner, its speakers crackling between joyful notes of Christmas carols and sleigh bells. The tree jiggled and hummed.

The humming stopped.

Agnes' head popped out from behind the tree. Specks of red tinsel contrasted against the white of her hair. After her almost fatal encounter with The Dark's Collector, Agnes had been tempted to restore it to its former blazing-red glory, but she was still recovering. Her magic was still weak, unable to draw any significant power from the Aether.

"I see you have new jewellery," she said.

Sally grinned. "A gift from the kids in the Children's Ward. They made it themselves." She rolled her wrist to display each bead in turn. "Spells out: 'thank you'."

"How was your shift?" Agnes stepped up onto the arm of the settee, tested her balance before catching a loop of red tinsel over a nail above the window, and draped it along the wall. "Not too many drunks, I hope."

"A lot of broken arms and concussions." Sally's duffle bag slid down her arm and dropped onto the armchair. "And idiots hanging Christmas decorations without a ladder."

"Yes, well…" Agnes stepped off the settee and brushed tinsel out of her hair.

"I thought Aunt Enid didn't do Christmas trees," said Sally.

"Alfred insisted." Agnes raised an eyebrow. "He brought everything over early this morning."

"And she agreed?"

Agnes nodded. "The 'no tree or decorations' was more a Sylvia thing. Said it was too frivolous; a distraction." She dusted off her skirt and sank into the settee. "After she passed, it sort of…" She adjusted a tree bauble tapping her on the shoulder. "We just never found the time. It's the summer heat. Plays havoc with connections between the worlds." She scoffed. "A few years back, a Howler led us a merry dance. Even had TV news crews chasing around the Hills."

"Howler?" asked Sally.

"A thylacine. Meddlesome creatures. Make a horrific noise. Stinks worse. Most of them retreated back to the Otherworlds. But every now and then—"

"We're in here, dear." Aunt Enid's cheerful voice drifted across the hallway.

Sally slipped her aunt's present under the tree next to the others, and peeked at the labels. One to her. One to her aunt.

Both from Agnes. And three more stacked behind them.

Agnes slapped her fingers. "You'll have to wait. Your aunt wants us all to open them together." She licked her lips. "Alfred made a Christmas cake."

"I didn't know Alfred was spending Christmas day with us."

Agnes smiled. "You've been busy at work." She leaned in close. "He's spending a lot of time here." She winked.

A low growl filtered across the hallway.

"Though I don't think Mr B is happy about it."

Bells tinkled as Sally stepped through the bead curtain into the kitchen. Mouth-watering aromas of coffee, ginger, and golden syrup tickled her nose. A thin layer of steam clung to the ceiling. A kettle bubbled on the enormous wood-burning stove, which dominated the far wall. Water spluttered and hissed on the hot plate.

The table in the centre of the room was dusted with flour. Aunt Enid peeled dough from its plastic wrapping and placed it on a lined baking tray, next to a dozen other naked gingerbread men.

Alfred stood beside her, whispering in her ear. Aunt Enid smiled. Mr B sat on a kitchen chair opposite, and glared at him, ignoring the strand of glittering silver tinsel caught over his ear.

Alfred caught Sally's eye, and dusted his hands on his apron. Aunt Enid busied herself setting four teacups and saucers on the table while Alfred retrieved a jar of honey from the pantry.

The kettle on the stove hissed.

"How was your day, Sally?" Enid hugged her.

"As eventful as yours, it seems," she replied. "It looks like the garden gnomes rioted in here." Sally scratched Mr B behind an ear. "I like the tree."

"Isn't it a beauty?" Alfred wiped the end of the table with the corner of his apron and placed the honey pot in front of Aunt Enid's favourite chair. "Though I'm not sure we should use the candle lights. There's an extreme fire hazard again today."

"I agree. This heat is unbearable" Sally slumped into the nearest chair and fanned her face.

"Long shift?" Aunt Enid removed the kettle from the stove and swirled some hot water in a teapot.

Sally nodded. She inhaled the comforting aromas of ginger and spices. Her great aunt's baking brought back childhood memories of long, hot summer holidays spent in this very house.

"You haven't made gingerbread since—" Images of animated garden gnomes marching across the front yard flashed in her memory. She hitched her breath.

Something tugged her skirt. Her heart raced. Her fingertips prickled.

"Sally?" A hand touched her arm.

Sally snapped out of the nightmare,

In the lounge room, the Christmas carols faded. The record hissed and crackled. A click, and the music started up again.

Her aunt stood by her. Mr B's tail twitched as he wove around her legs.

Sally clenched her fingers, and centred herself. "It reminds me of the school holidays I used to spend here."

Aunt Enid patted her shoulder. "It's Alfred's favourite."

Alfred grinned. "I didn't realise you celebrated Christmas," said Alfred.

"Why wouldn't we?" The bead curtain bells jingled as Agnes entered the kitchen.

"I… er..." Alfred's gaze flicked between the three women. "I just thought, since you're… with your magic and…"

Enid poured herself a cup of coffee. A smile flickered over her lips. Agnes removed another piece of red tinsel from her hair.

Alfred dusted off the rest of the table.

Sally pulled off one of her driving gloves and slapped it onto the table. The second stuck, the leather catching on her sweating skin.

"These gloves!" She yanked off the remaining glove. "I forgot them one day, last week. Just one, and the radio's been on the fritz ever since. And don't get me started on my mobile phone. Do you know how many I've had to replace? I ended up downgrading to a basic model so they'll last longer." She harrumphed. "Thank goodness I can't afford an electric car."

"I've got some tools in the boot. I can take a look at it, if you want." Alfred untied his apron. "I used to tinker with radios when I was younger."

Mr B pushed against Sally's calf. She flopped back in her chair and stroked his back. He arched his back and purred.

"That would be great." She shoved the glove in her pocket and retrieved a handful of toffees and her car keys. "Thanks." She handed him the keys and trickled all but two of the toffees into his hand. "A gift from one of our regulars in ED." She leaned closer and whispered, "I know you have a sweet tooth."

"Much appreciated." He grinned, and popped one into his mouth, and nodded. "Good as done."

He retrieved his jacket from the back of the kitchen chair. Silver metal glinted from one of the inside pockets as he folded it over his arm.

"Do you always carry those with you?"

"Yes."

"Isn't it illegal to carry lockpicks?" asked Sally. "I mean, your son is a police detective."

"Yes." Alfred held a finger to his lips. He removed them from his jacket pocket and slipped them inside his waistcoat. "Don't tell him; he'd have to charge me." He winked. "Then, I think I'll head down the hill to buy some tree lights. Shouldn't be long."

Aunt Enid frowned and shook her head.

"Electric lights would possibly be more dangerous," said Sally.

"Why?" asked Alfred.

Aunt Enid wiggled her fingers. Sparks rolled between them.

"Oh, right." Alfred placed his folded apron on the bench.

Mr B detached himself from Sally and followed Alfred to the kitchen doorway as if escorting him out.

"Now Alfred's gone, we need to talk." Agnes sat in the chair opposite Sally and poured her a cup of tea, then one for herself.

Aunt Enid joined them and cradled her cup in her hands.

Sally wrapped her fingers around the teacup handle and eyed her aunts. They avoided her gaze. Their serious countenances made her stomach drop. She swallowed. It was as if they were preparing for an intervention. "What did you want to talk to me about?"

Her aunt squirmed in the chair.

Agnes elbowed her. "You have to tell her."

"You've been so busy at the hospital recently; we haven't had a chance to sit down since…" her aunt began.

"Yes." Sally's grip tightened on the teacup handle. "You've already said that."

"Oh, for goodness' sake." Agnes rolled her eyes. "This is your first Christmas as Protector—"

"And…" Aunt Enid glared at Agnes. "And there's some things you need to know about this time of year…" She twirled her cup on its saucer.

Sally tapped the china cup in her hand with her fingernail.

"Between Christmas and New Year," Agnes continued.

"It's a strange time." Aunt Enid raised her teacup.

Sally turned her teacup slowly. "Twixtmas?"

"What-mas?" Aunt Enid's cup froze mid-air.

"Some people call it Twixtmas," replied Sally.

"Which people?" asked her aunt.

"It sounds made up," asked Agnes.

"I suppose it was. It's a thing," replied Sally. "It's big business."

"Ah, commercialism at its best," scoffed Agnes.

"Whatever you call it," said her aunt, "There's a reason why no one knows what day it is, what they're doing—"

"Or sometimes who they are." Agnes chuckled.

"It was only the one time," said Aunt Enid.

"Oh, and it was a good one," said Agnes.

"Well, it's still a potentially perilous time for this world," said Enid. "There are more Thin Places, and they're more permeable."

"Easier to cross. Even for non-Travellers," added Agnes. "There was a young man…" Agnes stared out the window.

"I remember him." Enid straightened the gingerbread men on the baking tray. "Spotty youth—"

"He was not spotty," whispered Agnes.

"Always hanging around the local shops. Rambling about ghosts and trolls. Fortunately, the locals thought he was crazy. He stumbled into a Thin Place, oh… decades ago. Haven't seen him since."

"Yes, well…" Agnes flicked the tinsel remnant from her hair into the bin. "It's crucial we're all on our guard, be careful with our magic on… Twixtmas."

"And it's a scorcher today. They've declared an extreme fire danger over the entire state. That makes it worse," said Agnes.

"But it's Christmas," said Sally. "You know: good will and all that."

"Here, yes ideally, but there's the Otherworlds to consider." Agnes' smile faded.

Mr B's ears pricked. He stared out the kitchen door.

"I thought you said we're protected by 'shells' or something?" Sally asked Agnes. "That the worlds were all separated."

"Usually," said her aunt.

"Like the Howler?" Sally placed her cup on the table. "Those connections you mentioned? They're opening?"

Aunt Enid nodded. "It can be unpredic—"

Mr B's ear twitched. A low growl rumbled in his throat.

Aunt Enid returned her cup to its saucer on the bench with a clunk, and scowled. "Behave yourself, Mr B. Alfred's our friend. You're just going to have to get used to the idea." She sighed, picked up the baking tray from the table. "The gingerbread won't cook itself," said Aunt Enid.

There was a scrape of metal outside.

Mr B's tail spiked. He launched himself into the hallway. The front screen door flapped.

Aunt Enid rolled her eyes and slipped the tray into the oven.

The bells on the bead curtain jangled as Mr B rushed back in from outside. He slid into Aunt Enid's shins and yowled.

"What the—"

A bright white light flashed through the window and splashed across the kitchen walls. It settled into an eerie, flickering blue glow.

Sally jumped to her feet. Her chair unbalanced and clattered onto the linoleum floor.

"Alfred!" Aunt Enid slammed the oven shut, snatched up her silver walking cane from the umbrella stand by the door, and rushed into the front yard.

Sally raced out after her, Agnes on her heels.

chapter three

The faint tinkle of bells on the kitchen's bead curtain inside slowed and faded as Sally stepped onto the verandah.

A wall of heat slammed her. Hydrangea petals fluttered and danced in the swirling wind. Dust eddies rose from bare patches in the loose-gravelled driveway. Scorching gusts caught her hair, dragging strands across her face as wind turned and raced along the side of the house, past the cars towards the back yard. A faint scent of wet woollen socks and stale herbs lingered.

Sleigh bells jingled faintly in the back yard.

The sky had taken on an unnatural, green tinge. Blurred shadows moved slowly above her, only a thin membrane separating the unknown terrors of the Otherworlds from this one.

A handful of agitated bees flitted around her head.

A loud crash echoed off the house and outbuildings, and along the protective shield created by the hawthorn fence.

The bees darted towards the noise.

The wooden gate rattled in warning.

Sally grabbed for the shovel she'd seen left near the doorway. Her fingers scraped sandstone. It was gone.

The screen door slapped behind her.

Agnes rushed past, her arm raised to shield her eyes from debris and dust of the growing gale, and ran towards the cars parked alongside the cottage.

"Alfred?" Enid's voice carried on the returning wind.

Sally pressed forward.

Her old, pale blue hatchback jostled and rocked, its metal screeching and groaning, and its open driver door swinging with each buffet of wind. The missing shovel lay twisted on the ground by the rear wheel of Alfred's BMW. She slammed the car door shut, and paused to retrieve it.

Alfred was nowhere in sight.

She ran a finger along a deep, jagged rent scarring the bonnet. "Where's Alfred?"

Agnes checked the far side of the car, shrugged her shoulders, and continued on.

Sally followed.

Enid's grey hair twisted around her neck as she turned full circle, searching the back yard for any sign of him. She held her walking cane in the air - like a sword - and swung it in an arc before her as if searching for something unseen.

In the centre of the yard, a swirling circle of shimmering blue-green light was suspended half a metre above the ground. Its throbbing light bathed over them.

Enid took a deep breath and walked slowly towards the portal.

It growled, and pulsed brighter.

She froze. Her grip tightened on the handle of her cane.

Sparks crackled around its edge, each surge generating

a sweet, tangy burst of ozone into the air. Shards of light twirled and glittered, revealing reflected glimpses of her aunt's cottage and laundry shed, alternating with flashes of unfamiliar vegetation and lilac sky from the Other side.

"Where's Alfred?" Agnes joined Enid.

Bees bobbed around Enid, as she stared into the dizzying kaleidoscope of light, silhouetted by the portal's radiance. She gulped, and ignored them. Deep furrows in her forehead betrayed her feelings.

Small ripples breached the portal's undulating surface. Dark spots formed in the centre of each one.

"Something's coming through." Sally edged closer. "Agnes?" She hesitated. "Is it safe?"

The ripples bulged and exploded. Several bees broke through and joined the others. They buzzed furiously around Enid's head. She batted them away.

Her eyes widened. "Pardon?" Her gaze flicked across the yard, then fixed on the portal. She shook her head.

"Alfred?" Her voice wavered as she stepped closer to the portal.

"Enid, wait up." Agnes closed in on Enid.

A blur of charcoal fur sped past Sally and deposited itself at her aunt's feet, dragging a line of silver tinsel behind him.

A few bees detached from the cluster and regrouped near Agnes. She held out her hand. One of the bees dropped gently on her palm and waggled in a figure eight, angling itself as it did so. It buzzed louder as it danced. She stooped to listen.

The remaining bees continued their discourse with Enid.

"He what?" Enid's voice rose in pitch, almost breaking.

Sally's muscles tensed.

Agnes cursed under her breath.

The bee on her hand launched into the air.

Enid staggered forward, almost tripping over Mr B as he curled tighter around her calves.

"Get out of my way." She pushed him away with the tip of her cane.

He turned as he staggered back, twisting the long strand of tinsel around his legs.

The bees swarmed in front of her.

"You, as well," she hissed.

"Enid, no!" The faint ruby glow of Agnes' Protector amulet flickered under her blouse. It sputtered and dimmed.

Her hand trembled as she grabbed Enid's arm. She steadied herself, and whispered in Enid's ear.

The sound of heavy marching feet thundered across the yard and echoed along the hawthorn hedge behind the portal, and from the gully beyond. A line of garden gnomes faced Enid and closed ranks to form a barrier between her and the portal.

Their black lidless eyes stared back at them.

At Sally.

Sally's heart plunged into her stomach. Her fingertips tingled. She turned each bead on the plastic bracelet on her wrist, counting them as she did so. Twenty in all. She inhaled a slow, deep breath.

Her aunt needed her.

She shook out her fingers and took a deep breath. She would not panic. At least, not yet.

A charcoal blur barrelled past Sally. She snatched at

the tinsel fluttering in Mr B's wake. He rolled free of its entanglement and stalked back towards her aunt.

Enid scooped something up from the ground, and stared at the portal.

Agnes whispered in her ear again. Quiet, soothing words. Enid's eyelids fluttered. The keys slipped from her hand; her finger caught in the ring. An enamelled daisy dangled from them.

Sally frowned. They were her car keys; the ones she had given Alfred so he could fix her car radio.

She scanned the area in front of the portal; there were no footprints. No sign of an altercation. And, more importantly: there was no blood. Alfred hadn't been injured; at least, not on this side of the portal.

She kicked a tuft of flattened grass. It was possible any traces had already been erased in the wild winds.

A glint of metal winked back at her; she retrieved a pocket-sized metal case: Alfred's lockpick kit. She peeled back the grass, to find a bent lockpick. Then another. Three in all.

Alfred was rarely parted from his picks; he wore them as a badge of honour. She suspected they were also an act of defiance against his caring, but over-protective son, a local police detective.

The picks clicked against each other in her hand. They were metal. Stainless steel… There was a memory… Something her aunt had said… Fae didn't like iron; it wreaked havoc with magic in the Otherworlds.

She slipped them back into their case before her aunt or Agnes noticed.

Another blast of wind buffeted her. Twigs of hawthorn

snapped and flew at the portal, exploding in bursts of sweet, nauseating scent.

Enid sniffed the air, tightening her grip on the keys as she spun to face the portal. Sally could smell it too: the same stench of old socks she'd smelled earlier.

Agnes' nose wrinkled.

"A Howler?" She stepped closer to the portal and ventured another sample of air.

"It must've dragged him through." Enid tugged her arm free of Agnes' grip.

Agnes shook her head. "Howlers aren't aggressive."

"But what if…" Enid fidgeted with the keys. "What if he's…" There was a flicker of panic in her eyes. Her attention snapped back to the portal's groaning surface.

Agnes touched her arm, and spoke in a quiet, soothing voice: "Alfred can look after himself."

"Nothing's come through." Sally pointed at the ground near the portal. "Look. There's no drag marks, and only one set of footprints going into the portal." She clutched the lockpick kit behind her back. "Everything will be fine, Auntie."

Agnes nodded slowly. "Yes, yes. Sally's correct."

Enid peered at the ground.

"What about on the other side?" The fear returned to her eyes. "He's an innocent. Without magic…" She swallowed. "He can't protect himself."

She lunged at the portal. A rumble of marching steps shook the ground as her garden gnomes closed ranks in front of her.

Wind swirled around her. It tugged at her dress, and flattened her cheeks. Her hand trembled. The keys slipped from her fingers and landed at Sally's feet.

Enid leaned forward, closer to the portal. Her amulet chain pulled tight on her neck.

"Enid, don't." Agnes tugged Enid back from the portal's rippling surface.

Enid pushed her away. "No, I must—"

"*Cessa!*" A sudden flash of ruby light burst from Agnes' amulet. Her voice boomed, bending the grass as the sound waves swept across the yard.

Sally's ears rang.

Enid froze, centimetres from the portal's surface.

The colour drained from Agnes' face. She swayed and reached out to steady herself.

"You know you can't go through. You're not a Traveller." She shook her head.

Enid turned slowly, as she loosened the chain around her neck and rubbed the angry, red mark encircling it.

"No Protector has ever… *must* ever travel through a portal," hissed Agnes.

"Never?" The discarded keys crunched under Sally's foot. She picked them up.

"It's forbidden." Agnes caught Enid's gaze as if to reinforce her words. "Remember?"

Enid eyed the darkened amulet at Agnes' neck. She narrowed her eyes. Their spark had returned. "It's not a normal portal."

Agnes released her hold on Enid's arm. Her voice remained firm: "You remember what happened last time."

"But this is different," Enid replied, "It's Twixtmas; the spheres have touched, creating an artificial Thin Place - one not used by Travellers." She fidgeted with the chain of her amulet.

That word again. *Travellers*. They'd mentioned it twice now. Sally eyed the two women and frowned. What were they not telling her?

Sally scuffed at the dry ground. There was another glint of silver. She bent down and parted the blades with her fingers, and picked up a fourth lockpick.

She eyed the long graze scarring the bonnet of Alfred's car, and then considered the contorted shovel deposited next to its tyre.

She rolled the items in her hand: the stainless steel lockpicks, the keys. All metal.

A theory was forming… If she was right, she had the best chance of surviving the crossing, and returning. She eyed the lockpick. She just had to test it.

"Traveller?" Sally stepped closer to the swirling light. Her amulet twitched under her blouse, and warmed against her skin. She stepped closer, careful to avoid the sentry line of garden gnomes. Her amulet jerked away from the portal; its metal chain bit into her skin.

"Only Travellers can pass through a portal safely," replied Agnes. "And Protectors aren't Travellers."

"Neither is Alfred," whispered Enid.

"It is forbidden for us to cross into an Otherworld," said Agnes.

"Not entirely correct." Enid flexed her fingers. "We *shouldn't* cross. It's not expressly stated we *can't*."

"And why do you think there's a rule, why it's forbidden?" asked Agnes.

"Since when do you follow the rules?" scoffed Enid.

Agnes' shoulders slumped. "I've already lost Olive."

"We've got Sally now," said Enid.

"What do you think…? Did you stop to consider how I—" She cleared her throat. "…how we'd cope if we lost you?"

Mr B wound around Enid's calves. His tail twitched. He nudged her away from the portal. Enid pushed him away as she traced her thumb across the faded, circular scar on her wrist, left by her own amulet over a hundred years earlier when she'd bonded with it.

"We can't leave him unprotected, in an unknown world." Enid took a step closer to the portal. "I have to protect him. Who knows what dangers he'll face."

"Auntie, please. Don't." The wind snatched away Sally's voice. snatched away on the wind

"I won't lose you," growled Agnes.

The guard of gnomes snapped to attention in front of her. The ground resounded under their feet. Sally's stomach churned.

Agnes rested one hand on her chest, over her amulet. "We need you here." Her fingers blanched. She stared directly into Enid's eyes. "You don't need to follow Alfred."

Enid flinched.

Agnes' skin faded to an ashen colour. Her amulet's ruby light faded. Her breath faltered. She leaned heavily on Sally; she'd used what little power she had left in her attempt to save Enid.

Enid glared at Agnes, her breathing slow and measured.

"We're Protectors. It's our duty to protect the innocent," she hissed.

"Yes, it's *our* duty." Sally stepped past them.

Red barred her.

The air stilled around her. She was entering the eye of the storm. The portal's surface slowed, allowing brief, tantalising glimpses of the Otherworld beyond. The image shimmered. A glade, ringed by trees, tinged blue and yellow. In the distance, smoke rose in the distance into a violet sky filled with dark pink clouds.

She removed a lockpick from its case and poked the surface with it. Sparks spat over her.

"Don't," Agnes scolded. "It's not safe. We don't know what lurks on the other side."

There was a tug. Resistance. The pick flung out of Sally's hand.

Agnes cursed, and yanked Enid out of its path.

The pick landed with a crack on the BMW's windscreen, bounced, and embedded itself into the bonnet. Sally winced. Alfred wouldn't be happy.

She eyed the rejected pick, then the ragged gash along the bonnet and the twisted shovel, which had caused the damage. She let the keys dangle, and held out her hand. They swung away from the portal. She let go. They flew away from the portal and clattered onto the car.

"It's metal." Sally whispered under her breath.

"Pardon?" asked Agnes.

"I'll go," she replied, louder.

"I won't let you risk yourself." Enid tucked her amulet back under her blouse.

• "It has to be me." Sally removed her watch and handed it to Agnes. "The lockpick is metal. So is the spade, and my keys. They're all metal."

Her Protector amulet warmed her skin under her shirt. A pale blue light grew at its centre. She unhooked it, and dangled it in the air. Its polished silver glistened in the throbbing light. At its heart was a large, glowing sapphire, now dimming with each erratic surge of Otherworldly light. It jiggled on the end of its chain, slowly rose into the air, and tugged trying to escape. "The portal rejects metal."

The surface shuddered, its colours shifting and dimming for a second.

Agnes' eyes widened. She gripped Sally's wrist and shook her head. "No."

Agnes had realised her plan.

"We're not losing anyone." Sally patted Agnes' arm.

Enid grabbed Sally's wrist. "I forbid it." She, too, had realised Sally's intent. "Without a Focus - without magic - you can't protect yourself, let alone anyone else."

"Which is why I must go," said Sally.

"You can't." Enid frowned. "The portal is unstable"

"I'm the only one who has a chance. You know it. Agnes knows it."

"That doesn't mean I have to like it." Enid removed her hand from Sally's wrist.

Sally removed her driving glove from her pocket and slipped the amulet inside. A shiver flicked up her spine. She felt naked without it.

"You both need a Focus to channel your magic. I saved Alfred before, without it I can do it again. I have the best chance." She swallowed, and pressed it into her aunt's hand "Let me do this for you, Auntie."

The bees returned to Enid. They buzzed quietly as they hovered close to her ear. She clenched her fists, and nodded.

While her fellow Protectors were distracted, she took a step back. And another. Slowly, so not to alert them. They mustn't stop her. It was her fault Alfred was trapped in an Otherworld, with unknown dangers; it was *her* car radio, he'd been trying to fix. And if, as her aunt had said, they needed magic to survive on the other side, neither of them could channel the Aether's power without their Focus, and the metal required to do so.

A strong wind pressed against her back. She leaned into it. Another step. Closer to the portal.

"You've done so much for me," she continued, her voice calm. "I have to do this. For you both. I—" The wind caught Sally's words; she was close to the portal now.

Another march-step of the garden gnome army alerted Enid. She thumped the tip of her walking cane on the ground.

"*Cessa!*" Her voice boomed across the back yard.

Sally froze.

The bees retreated behind Enid. Agnes stiffened.

"Alfred is my responsibility. You both are." Enid clenched her fists tighter.

Mr B curled closer around her calves, holding her back.

"Trust me, Auntie." Sally placed her hand over her aunt's clenched fist. "It's what family does. We protect each other. And Alfred's practically family now."

The bees rallied around Enid, filling the air with a soft, calming hum. Slowly, her aunt's fists relaxed.

Enid's shoulders slumped. Her eyes met Sally's. There was fear there; only a sliver of grey rimmed her dilated pupils. Tears welled along the rims of her eyelids.

Sally couldn't fail; she had to save Alfred or it might destroy her aunt.

Enid lowered her gaze. "But only if Red takes a squad with you. Gnomes are natural Travellers. They will protect you, and the bees will show you the way."

Sally's heart thumped. Images of gnome-shaped shadows flashed through her mind. Cold fingers pawed at her calves and crawled up her legs. Her leg muscles tensed; she wanted to run, but the portal blocked her escape.

The gnomes will protect me. She squeezed her eyes shut, and twisted each bead on the plastic bracelet, trying to banish the nightmare. *They're on our side. Red will protect me.*

A soft, comforting buzz caressed her ear. *The bees will warn me of danger.* She smiled and opened her eyes.

A tear trickled down Enid's cheek. Her hands shook. "And Sally…" she took a deep breath as if to reassure herself. "To be safe: be careful not to eat anything."

Sally nodded and turned to face the portal. Shards of light danced across its surface, reflecting the concerned faces of the two women holding each other tight. Glimpses of the Otherworld on the far side - with its striking vegetation and lavender sky - winked at her. It didn't look too scary. Perhaps the past Protectors had been overly cautious in their warnings?

She drew in a slow, deep breath, savouring the familiar scents of home, as she approached the portal.

The hairs along her arms, and at the back of her neck, pricked. Her stomach twisted into a complex of knots, and tightened.

She counted the beads on her bracelet. ...*Nineteen... twenty.*

Her pulse slowed. Her heart fluttered. This time, there was a hint of excitement. She was likely the first Protector to cross into the Otherworlds.

Half a dozen bees entered first, swallowed up by the

kaleidoscope of blue, lavender, and green reflected light.

Red stood by her.

Sally's skirt fluttered, its weight dragging her forward. A rush of wind pushed - no pulled - her towards the vortex. Shards of light tumbled and glinted, like spinning daggers, their tips pricking her skin.

Her heart thumped, sinking into her chest as she stepped up into the portal. Heat flashed over her skin.

"And don't trust everything you see." Her aunt's voice trailed off. The portal's ravenous groan swelled around her.

The faint jingle of Christmas bells echoed in her ears, as the last notes of Christmas music were drowned out by the lingering hum of buzzing bees in the void. The buzz grew louder, rising in pitch. A piercing scream scraped her nerves as every cell in her body was ripped apart and then smashed together.

A firm hand clasped hers.

She was not alone.

chapter four

A thousand burning knives twisted in Sally's gut. They pushed deeper, slicing into her spine.

She fell forward, further into the darkness. Shafts of blue and green light flickered in her vision. Her ears rang, the portal's low growl almost lost in the constant hiss reverberating through her skull.

Sally's knees slammed hard against resistance. Pain shot through her forearm. Tears filled her eyes.

The jingle of sleigh bells filled the air, for a brief moment. Snippets of carol singers followed - both swallowed by the raging wind as it twisted her hair across her face.

Long sharp ribbons whipped her skin, tapping her arms and legs in the total blackness; unseen foes crawling over her body. Sally squeezed her eyes tight, trying not to imagine a horde of garden gnomes, their soulless eyes assessing her, their imagined whispers replacing the ringing: *failure*.

The ribbons clung to her, needling deep into her skin. Her fingers recoiled.

Another burst of pain seared along the bone of her forearm. She shifted to try to ease the pain, and ventured a slow, steady breath.

The air tasted different. Odd.

The gnomes were ceramic constructs, with no need for air, but she… Was this Otherworld's atmosphere even breathable for humans?

Sally held her breath. She hadn't thought this through: jumping into a mysterious portal, of origins unknown, after a ceramic garden ornament. What was she thinking? Would she succumb to a noxious atmosphere before she could find Alfred?

Her lungs burned.

And if… when she found him, would he be…?

She gulped for air. The sweet tang of freshly crushed grass and wet soil filled her nostrils. Granules caught in her throat. Her lungs heaved, coughing up the foreign particles. Pain shuddered through her chest.

Sally gritted her teeth. Where were the garden gnomes - the small army her aunt had promised would protect her?

Pain buzzed along her right arm. Her fingers tingled. Sally clenched her hand and cursed under her breath.

Calm. Remain calm.

She relaxed her fist and reached out, slowly feeling the ground around her with her other hand. The spiky ribbons lifted as she moved her hands in an arc around her.

Something soft and silky brushed against her skin. She ran her fingers over its frayed edges. Possibly a remnant of fabric? She clutched it in her hand, and continued her search, but there was no sign of the garden gnomes. What if they were stuck in the portal? Was she…?

Sally's pulse raced.

The portal groaned behind her, sucking in the air, and

dragging her backwards towards it.

Then silence.

Muffled voices broke through its surface.

A boom, and the air surged back, pushing her forward, face-first onto the ground. Sharp pricks needled her cheeks. Moisture dripped down Sally's neck, and drizzled under her collar.

The portal roared again. Wind howled around her legs, its chill cutting to her bones. She shivered. Her fingers caught on the damp cotton as she pulled her thin, summer skirt around her.

Sally pushed herself off the ground. Her arms trembled. An agonising howl reverberated through her skull; her scream, piercing the persistent ringing in her ears. She rolled onto her left side and struggled back onto her knees.

Sparks flared in her peripheral vision, consuming the darkness. Blotches of violet and red light coalesced. She blinked, but the world remained a blurred mass of colours.

Her stomach heaved, hurling up its contents, burning her oesophagus as it erupted onto the ground before her. The knives in her gut pushed deeper into her spine. Slowly, her vision cleared; the blue, yellow, and red smudges resolved into strange forms of gnarled, misshapen vegetation and an unfamiliar lavender sky dotted with enormous dark pink clouds rimmed with light from two blazing blurs in the sky.

A glade of long, yellow grass swirled around her, twirling and twisting in the chaotic wind of the portal's wake. It whipped her bare arms, its sharp, fur-like covering embedding into her skin.

A bee hovered at the edge of the flattened area of grass, which surrounded her. It buzzed gently. The tightness in her muscles eased. She wasn't alone.

Sally opened her clenched fist and examined the scrap she'd found; red satin.

"Where's Red?" she asked.

The bee turned to face a line of trees in the distance. It waggled its abdomen, and hesitated.

Sally parted the blades of grass and examined the soft, wet ground. A faint shoeprint was visible in the soil.

"Alfred?"

The bee hummed in reply.

Sally nodded.

Her new companion darted off in search of the garden gnome. She tucked the scrap of material into her skirt pocket and rose to follow.

The world contorted around her. She stumbled forward; her foot caught, and slipped out of her sandshoe. She tumbled back to the ground, landing on her wrists. The pain in her right arm doubled as sharp shards buried into her palms.

Several flat stones lay scattered over the area. Thin, cold, and curiously curved. A multitude of colours: white, black, green, blue, and red.

Sally picked up one of the shards - blue on the curved side, white on the convex. Possibly ceramic? She tested its edge: razor-sharp. She winced as it fell. It clinked on another shard, and skittered into the grass, landing with a soft thud.

Definitely ceramic. Some of her garden gnome guard hadn't made it through the portal.

She sucked her finger. The metallic taste of fresh blood confirmed it had sliced the skin. But there was more. A bitter taste. She screwed up her nose, and spat out the sappy liquid.

Sally flipped over another shard. *Red*. It looked like…

Her heart sank. Its shape resembled the tip of a cap.

Sally swallowed. She had no knowledge of this world, of any Otherworld. How could she find Alfred without a guide? And she needed a Traveller to get back home. She'd be stuck here forever. Alone.

She lifted her head and searched the glade. There was no sign of Red, her new bee companion, or Alfred.

Away from the portal, the wind was less hectic; a soft breeze rippled across the long grass, creating a sea of yellow lapping at the ring of trees, with dark leaves tinged with orange and red, surrounding the glade.

"Red!" Her voice echoed off the trees.

A faint, deep moan rolled across the glade, as if in reply. A large hairy quadruped stood half way across the glade. It raised its head for a moment, then returned to grazing.

A glint of pale yellow bobbed and dodged its way through the grass, moving towards her.

Sally froze. Any sudden movement could make it attack. Her breath hitched. If it'd already attacked Red, what chance did she have?

Her hand twinged. She rubbed away dark red beads. Could it smell her blood? Was it carnivorous?

She ducked, lowering her head just enough so she could see over the quivering grass - too late if the creature had already caught her scent.

Aunt Enid had told her the bees would lead the way; they'd warn her of danger.

Where was that damned bee? She searched the glade. There was no sign of her new companion. Surely, it would have returned to warn her if there was danger?

The yellow-haired creature submerged into the grass.

Sally's muscles tensed, preparing for attack, wishing Red were here, with her. It was a strange feeling: preferring the company of a garden gnome - the source of many nightmares - but this was a strange world and she desperately wished not to be on her own.

She pressed the cuts on her hands to staunch the blood as she scanned the grass in a circle around her, looking for any sign of the creature.

Her fingertips throbbed. How could she survive in the Otherworlds without her protector?

"Shut up," she hissed under her breath. "You can handle the Emergency Room on a Friday night; you can handle this." She inhaled a long breath through her nose. Perhaps she could follow the shoeprints? She just had to move, to find a new sanctuary.

Sally glanced back at the portal, for what could be the last time. Its colours had taken on the purple hue of the Otherworld sky. Triangles of light tumbled slowly, providing the occasional glimpse of her two aunts, and fellow Protectors, consoling each other, alternating with flashes of Alfred's BMW.

Sally's heart skipped. *Alfred*: the reason why she'd risked the journey. She had to find him. But how? And where?

The bees will show you the way; it was as if her aunt's voice echoed through the portal. If she didn't have her guide, then she'd have to find the bees.

She squeezed her hand tighter and edged away from the portal.

A rustle.

Too close.

Sally's heart raced. She squeezed her hand tighter and scanned the nearby glade.

Another rustle.

She spun in the direction of the noise.

The portal groaned ominously behind her, the ferocity of its tempest whipping hair across her cheek. She peeled a damp strand from her eyes.

A flushed figure burst out of the grass, its face just centimetres from her eyes.

Sally recoiled, slipped on the wet grass, and landed on her wrists. Pain shot up her right arm. Blades of grass buried deep into the cuts on her palm.

She sucked in a sharp breath and scrabbled further back, increasing the distance between them.

Metal clinked as the creature stepped into the flattened area of grass surrounding the portal. Heavy black boots crushed the grass, creating bursts of crisp, sharp aroma. Silver buttons glinted on its deep-crimson leather coat dotted with water stains from the drizzling rain. A roll of scarlet wool was strapped to his back with two thin ropes. Hints of silver armour glinted under the coat.

In its heavy-gloved hands rested an over-sized, two-edged axe, almost as tall as the creature itself. Shoulder-length yellow hair framed its face. Dark, blank eyes stared directly at her, their pupils barely visible.

A shiver tracked down Sally's spine.

The creature cocked its head, and lowered its axe.

"Are you injured?" Its voice was soft and deep, easing the tension in her muscles slightly.

The creature lifted her chin, turned her head, and studied her eyes. "Are you… with us?"

Sally searched for an escape. Her legs were twice as long; surely, she could outrun it.

The creature frowned. It tugged a red cloth from its belt, removed a remnant of green tinsel, and shoved it on its head. The cap's peak drooped to one side.

Sally blinked. "Red?"

Fine lines formed at the edges of his eyes as the gnome smiled.

"Yes, Protector."

"You're not—?" Sally's shoulders relaxed. "I thought you were…"

"No, Protector."

"Then those shards aren't…"

"No, Protector," replied the gnome. "But we are without reinforcements."

She flung her arms around his shoulders. Her right forearm twinged. She gritted her teeth, trying to ignore the increasing pain.

His body stiffened under her embrace.

 "And, it's Sally," she said.

"Yes, Prot—" Armour shifted under his coat. "Yes, Protector Sally."

"Just Sally." She lowered her arms.

"Noted." He stepped back.

Sally retrieved the scrap of red silk from her pocket and presented it to him. "I thought I'd lost you."

He eyed the remnant. "My clothing is undamaged," he replied as he took her right wrist and rolled it over to inspect it.

Pain cut deep through her bone. She winced; she was sure something had shifted in her forearm.

She clenched her teeth as he slowly turned her wrist back.

"Are you injured?" he asked.

Sally's arm throbbed. For all her aunt's talk of the dangers of metal and portals, she'd still forgotten the surgical plate in her arm. Her great aunt's *Memory Magic*, cast decades ago, had manipulated her recollections. After recently discovering her aunt was a Protector with an army of garden gnomes at her command, fragments had slowly returned. Now the enchantment was fading completely.

Memories resurfaced: the sound of marching feet, the outlines of dark shapes rolling over the yard - over her body. Memories of struggling to breathe. Of bones breaking. She clutched her arm. Her great aunt - her own blood - had taken those memories from her.

She felt along the bone, noting each screw was still aligned, and flexed her fingers. Nothing broken, but it would need attention when she returned home.

"Are you injured?" he repeated.

"An old injury." She rubbed her arm. "Nothing I can't handle."

His eyes narrowed. "If you insist."

Rain dripped onto Sally's face as she nodded.

She eyed the creature before her: the leader of her great aunt's formidable army of ceramic garden ornaments, all with rimless, black eyes. Here he was: flesh and blood. And his eyes were still...

A wave of panic swept over her. Her fingertips tingled.

She inhaled a long, slow breath and began the mantra: *five things you can see.*

One: pupils barely visible within black irises.

Blood pounded in her ears.

But there was something else; a hint of compassion in the faint smile lines surrounding them. *That's two.*

The top of his red cap flapped - *three* - as he spoke to her, his voice drowned out by the rush of her pulse. She hitched her breath. *Four*.

He was real. Not a construct.

She concentrated on the carotid pulse in his neck, imagining the blood coursing through his veins, the thump of his heart. She counted the beats, as she would a patient: slow, steady, rhythmic. Her own pulse steadied, and slowed with it.

Five.

The tingling in her fingers faded.

The not-garden gnome stared at her, staring at him. She cleared her throat.

"Are all garden gnomes real?" she asked.

He shifted his stance, glanced past her, scanning the glade behind her, but didn't reply.

"I mean, here in the Otherworlds." She tucked a strand of damp hair behind her ear.

He raised an eyebrow. A smile touched the corners of his lips.

"No." He planted the haft of his great axe on the soft ground.

A faint sound of tinkling bells caught in the wind around them. Not from the portal. No, higher.

"Christmas bells? Here?" she whispered.

The gnome gripped his axe tighter and searched the sky.

Sally saw nothing but the low, rolling pink clouds,

rimmed with red, drifting across the lavender sky.

"We need to find cover. There's no telling what your scream has attracted." He pointed across the glade. "We can find shelter in the trees." His attention still fixed on the sky, he extended a gloved hand in her direction. A hand of flesh and blood encased in black leather, not painted ceramic.

Sally hesitated. She barely knew this gnome. Besides, if it was indeed her great aunt's garden gnome General and not an Otherworldly deceit, her aunt was the one who had adventures; she'd just tagged along for the ride.

He stretched out his fingers, as if to hurry her on.

Still, she held back.

Aunt Enid had vouched for him. He was her guide. Yet, she couldn't shake the haunting images: the flashes of dark, pupil-less eyes and crunching feet playing through her memory.

Sally tested her weight, first on her right leg, then the other. At least they seemed to be functioning. She flicked her soaked skirt off her ankles and pushed herself to her feet as a lone bee flew in to join them.

It buzzed around the gnome's head.

The gnome grasped her arm. "Wait."

He pulled her below the grass line.

The bee continued its report.

He nodded, placed his axe on the ground within reach, and removed a leather pouch from under his coat. Inside were two polished glass lenses - one convex, the other concave.

He unstrapped the leather brace from his arm and threaded the pouch's cord through a series of holes along the long edge of the bracer, then inserted a lens in grooves, one at each end of the bracer, and tightened the cord, pulling the leather into a tube.

He motioned to her to remain hidden as he lifted his spyglass above the grass line.

The bee swooped lower, hovering at his shoulder.

The gnome turned slowly, scanning the area, then froze.

He ducked down, cradling the spyglass on his lap, snatched up his axe, and hefted it in both hands.

The bee buzzed quietly. He frowned and whispered back, ignoring her.

Sally snatched the spyglass from his lap, and searched the glade. Rain drops slid down the lens.

A large field of the sticky, yellow grass stretched for a few kilometres in every direction, the groaning portal seething at its centre. Deep purple shadows crept over them as clouds tracked across the sky. Enormous cow-like quadrupeds covered in long, bile-coloured hair, the grass barely reaching their knees, dotted the glade where it rose in a gentle hill.

A lush forest ringed the glade. The vegetation was not unlike that of home, but in fantastic colours. Further in the distance, beyond the forest, a line of smoke rose into the sky.

A flurry of bees emerged from the edge of the tree line and sped towards them.

A long wail reverberated through the forest. The trees trembled.

The hair lifted on Sally's neck. Whatever her scream attracted, it was huge. She tensed, ready to run.

The bees dashed towards them, skimming low, just above the grass, and descended into their flattened sanctuary. They darted around Sally's head, their urgent buzzing drowning out the portal's low rumble.

Danger. Leave.

"Red?" Sally's voice squeaked.

He was already on his feet, brandishing his battle axe in both hands.

Another shadow slid over them. A tinkle of bells rang above.

"We must go," the gnome growled.

Sally swallowed. Her arm throbbed; it would need medical attention on their return home. She gathered the weight of her soaked skirt in her uninjured hand and prepared to run.

The gnome's eyes darted across the flattened grass. He motioned towards her discarded sandshoes. "You will need those."

Sally grabbed them. Lace remnants dangled from the shredded holes where the eyelets had been forcibly ripped out, rejected by the portal. She yanked out the fragments and slipped them back on her feet.

Her mind raced. She studied the trees at the edge of the glade. It didn't look far, judging by size of the *not*-cows. She could make it.

Their bee companions buzzed frantically, their voices overlapping as they darted around Sally's head.

She shook her head, and waved them away. "One at a time!"

"We need to leave." The gnome waded into the tall grass. "Now!"

chapter five

The bees led the way across the glade towards the cover of the trees. The gnome's woollen roll bounced on his back as he trotted after them, quickly consumed by the rolling waves of the long, yellow grass.

Sally followed. Blades of grass clung to her skirt, dragging it back as she moved forward. She caught up its hem to avoid the sticky barbs, and tracked his red cap as it bobbed through the grass.

Behind them, the portal's growl slowly faded, overwhelmed by sounds of the local fauna.

The gnome moved swiftly, apparently unhindered by the bothersome vegetation. Sally hurried after him, trying not to lose sight of his red cap. Each time it broke the grass's surface, he scanned the sky, not once breaking his stride.

A clicking chitter erupted at the edge of the forest. A flock of bird-like creatures the size of eagles danced at the edge of the trees. Their huge, transparent wings glistened pink and orange in the sunlight as they drifted across the glade. A flurry of shadows raced above her as they swooped and circled, their wings humming, then flitted towards the portal.

A distant, low bellow rolled over a gentle rise in the glade to her left. A rumbling bray replied. A cascade of replies followed, all in different tones.

Silence.

Then a higher-pitched cry, and a final response - a sharp bray of admonishment - and the herd continued with a gentle, communal braying.

A bank of dark red clouds peeked over the horizon and rolled over the forest towards them. The sky dimmed to a sombre mauve.

Sally shivered.

The portal's whine was faint now. Wind whistled over the top of the grass, whipping it against Sally's legs.

The air chilled.

A booming crack sounded behind her.

Sally's attention snapped back to the portal. Wind belched from its surface. Grass leaned towards the back surface as if being inhaled by its swirling vortex.

She turned back to follow her guide. There was no sign of him, or his red cap.

She waded to the top of the nearby rise. Clumps of bushes dotted the glade. The herd of creatures - not dissimilar to massive, hairy cows - was now visible, congregated under a stand of trees with wide, flat canopies of yellow and blue-tinged leaves. The older beasts had curved horns in the middle of their foreheads, long enough to skewer a human. Long tails, twice the creatures' length, with a tuft on the end, twitched in the air. Blades of the sticky, yellow grass clung to their long, tan hair.

A swarm of the glistening flying creatures swooped them. The *Not-Cows* flicked their long, tufted tails to shoo them away.

Sally scanned the remaining expanse of the glade for the gnome's familiar red cap. But there was still no sign of the gnome.

The forest was just over a kilometre away, ringing the edge of the glade. Its taller trees towered, casting deeper shadows on the maroon bushes below.

Beyond the forest, faint wisps of grey smoke rose into the sky.

A biting wind shook the treetops. Dark red clouds gathered. Lightning rimmed their edges in brilliant amethyst. Engorged raindrops fell onto the grass. Blades bent and sprang back as rain dripped and thudded onto the ground beneath

Thunder clapped above her.

The *Not-Cows* erupted into song again, and jostled each other into the cover of the trees.

Shadows rippled over the glade, their shapes unrecognisable in the moving grass.

Sally paused, scanning the grass around her.

She slowed to track the movements of the clouds above her, reconciling each one with its shadow, as it passed above her.

Then silence.

Sleigh bells tinkled faintly in the distance.

But the portal's groan was barely audible now; surely, she was too far away to hear Agnes' Christmas tunes. She shook her head; her ears were playing tricks on her.

The slow, soft braying of the *Not-Cows* grew louder. A calf fidgeted, its high-pitched cry barely heard above the constant chittering of the flying creatures swarming amongst them.

Swoosh.

The forest canopy shuddered. Leaves rustled louder as they began to sway furiously along a line towards the glade.

A resounding flap.

The birds squawked.

Then another. A large shadow separated from the trees, speeding towards her.

The *Not-Cows* stomped. The birds' screeching hitched. They rose into the air, turned suddenly and retreated into the trees.

Sally froze. The shadow was distinctly un-cloud-like. She shaded her eyes and squinted into the twin-sunned sky: nothing visible, other than the now fast-moving clouds pushed by an oncoming storm.

A sudden burst of air forced her to her knees, crushing her from above.

Another faint ring of—

Definitely sleigh bells. Directly above her.

The massive shadow circled.

Jingle.

She'd definitely heard it that time.

"Get down!" The gnome's voice was close.

Sally dropped into the grass; blades prickled her face and caught on her lips.

The shadow retreated upwards, its outline becoming visible with the extra distance - a massive creature with a wingspan twice its length. It sped towards the portal, picking up speed as it skimmed the grass, and slammed into its surface.

The portal erupted with a crackling explosion of light, bursting into life with a blaze of seething glare and sizzling smoke.

The shadow flickered and disappeared in the smoke.

The portal rumbled.

A deafening crack roared over the glade, flattening the grass.

A trail of frothing fumes surged over the grass, cloaking the creature. It shed smoke as it rebounded across the glade, until only a flickering shadow betrayed its trajectory.

Directly towards her!

A chill flashed over Sally's skin.

Her heart raced. She had to get to the cover of the trees.

She sprinted towards the forest. Blades whipped her skin, as she blundered through the grass.

Her sandshoe slipped off her foot. She tripped on the shoe and fell forward, face-first into the mud.

Pain shot up her right arm.

The steady flap of wings came closer.

Sally flung her arms over her head and lay still, praying the unseen creature would ignore her. She had no other choice.

The grass trembled.

A dark shadow engulfed her. Another downdraft pinned her harder into the ground, pressing on her chest.

She squeezed her eyes shut.

Don't move.

Her breath caught in her throat. Her lungs felt like they'd burst. White spots flashed over her vision.

The shadow faded.

The pressure on her chest eased.

Sally gasped for breath, and waited, not daring to move in case it was a trick.

Her skin itched. The grass's sharp smell filled her nostrils. Its sap clung to her like sweat. It dripped off her forehead and stung her eyes. She could taste it. She spat out the bitter sap, and strained to listen.

Again, silence.

She clutched her throbbing arm and rolled onto her back. With a growl, she flicked off her remaining shoe and threw it at the other one.

Sally's vision blurred. Her head spun, her pulse raced, and her fingers tingled.

She swallowed. She *had* to get to the forest. To safety.

To find the gnome. Who was supposed to protect her.

She cursed. Where was he?

Sally fidgeted with the plastic beads on the bracelet on her injured wrist, counting each bead to calm herself.

Another peal of thunder rumbled overhead.

A guttural caw croaked in the distance, barely audible above the storm. It grew louder. Closer.

She wiped rain from her eyes and peeked above the grass. Hair dripped on her shoulders and soaked her dress.

A jumble of claws, beak, and white feathers rushed at her. A flurry of white flashed in her face.

An alabaster bird, with a wingspan as wide as her outstretched arms, stared at her. It loomed over, its pink eyes gleaming, despite the shadow.

Its raised throat hackles quivered as it croaked. It pushed closer, its cry louder, more insistent.

"Go away," Sally glanced up at the sky, searching for the shadow creature.

Her fingers twitched. Heat flashed over her skin. A slow, loud flap drove rain against her face.

A dark shadow descended around her… and the jingle of sleigh bells.

She slammed hard against the ground and shrank back into the grass.

The creature had returned.

The bird shrieked. There was a sudden burst of wind, and the shadow creature was gone.

Sally's blood chilled.

A magnificent white raven hovered in front of her, the only clear focal point in her otherwise blurred vision.

"Thank you," said Sally.

It cocked its head, and replied with a series of gentle rattles and clicks. It drifted away until it blurred around the edges.

Sally didn't move. The raven halted. Its throat hackles puffed. It cawed loudly and darted closer.

Sally flinched.

Its voice pattern changed; the caws became a series of clicks.

"I don't understand."

Her thoughts were fuzzy, like her vision. Did it want her to follow it? To where? Could she trust it? Aunt Enid warned her not to trust anything.

She rose to one knee, staying below the grass line for cover, and scanned the glade. Everything was one big blur of smudged colours.

She either stayed put - in plain sight if the creature returned - or followed the raven in the hope it would lead her to safety.

Her head throbbed. She swallowed - her throat dry. What choice did she have?

"I need to find my—" What should she call the gnome? "My guide." She glanced back up at the dark sky. There was no chance to pick out the creature's shadow now. "I can't stay here."

Again, it pressed close and, again, it retreated.

"You want me to follow you?"

The bird croaked and nodded.

Sally stumbled forward, following the pale blur of her new guide, all the while listening for the telltale ring of bells and the flap of monstrous wings.

A speck of red surfaced above the yellow grass to her right. Footsteps thudded at the edge of her hearing.

"Here, quickly. This way before the creature returns."

"Red?" Her voice cracked.

He'd found her.

The raven continued ahead, in the opposite direction, away from the storm.

Sally hesitated. Which one could she trust? The raven had saved her from the shadow creature… She twisted the beads on her bracelet. But her aunt *had* vouched for the gnome.

She took a deep breath and flicked a strand of damp hair off her face, and followed the gnome until a wall of blurred, maroon trees loomed before her. Barely two hundred metres away.

Not far now.

Sally halted. There was no sign of the gnome's scarlet cap.

Another wave of heat flashed over her skin. Her legs ached. Her right forearm throbbed, and her head felt as vague as the fuzzy trees ahead of her.

A wave of exhaustion overwhelmed her. She dragged her

feet forwards, each step more difficult than the last.

Red? The name caught in her dry throat, emerging as a high-pitched squeak. Where the hell was he?

She lumbered towards the spot she'd last seen the gnome's cap, and halted. At her feet lay a small, hairless, rodent-like creature with a small snout, long whiskers, and oversized ears. Its skin was tinged orange. A feeling of dread settled in her chest; the same colour as the sap smeared over her own skin.

She clasped her aching arm. How had she missed the symptoms: blurred vision, dry mouth, heavy limbs? She should have realised. It wasn't exhaustion; the sap was toxic.

Sally felt ill. She slumped to the ground.

Shit! She slammed her fist into the mud.

And the bloody gnome had abandoned her. Again.

So much for trust. She'd have words with Aunt Enid when she got back home.

The faint tinkle of sleigh bells caught her ear. She shuddered.

If she got back home.

She rolled onto her side and pushed herself to her feet. Adrenaline could be a useful thing.

A dark shadow bathed over the grass surrounding her.

She flung her head back and raised her arm to shield herself.

A blurred silhouette separated from the grass.

Sally struggled to stand.

More bells.

Her head reeled. The world whirled. She lost her balance and toppled in a confusion of limbs. Strong arms grabbed her shoulders and cushioned her fall.

The last thing she heard was the gnome's voice: "I have you," and the low, guttural caw of a raven.

chapter six

Sweat rolled down Sally's nose. A bitter aftertaste lingered in her dry throat.

She groaned. Too much of Aunt Enid's trifle always gave her nightmares.

A bird chittered above her.

She rolled onto her back. The scent of fresh, wet moss and soap enveloped her. Her head swam, and took a few seconds to catch up.

Agnes had definitely spiked it.

She moaned and cradled her head in her hand. She wasn't a fan of sherry.

Her skin burned where she touched it. She grimaced. And she'd fallen asleep on the garden lounge again.

She cracked open one eye.

Glints of purplish-red flickered through the leaves overhead. It was later than she thought. Her eye muscles ached as she attempted to refocus her vision.

Bang. Crack!

The sounds reverberated through her skull.

She tried to sit up.

Big mistake.

Her head whirled, and her stomach heaved. She threw herself forward just in time, and wiped her chin. The sour taste clung to the back of her throat.

Pain twisted along her right ulna and radius. She'd have to raid Aunt Enid's medicine cabinet as soon as she wrangled this hangover.

She opened her eyes. Reluctantly.

Shafts of fading sunlight pierced through a woven ceiling of thin branches.

Her heart sank. *Not on the sun lounge.*

She reached out to investigate her surroundings.

"Red?" her voice cracked. She retched, and swallowed back another wave of vomit.

The bees drone increased in pitch.

"Protector?" A soft, deep voice.

A chill flashed over her skin, followed by a wave of heat. The creature by her elbow came into focus: short, yellow hair, dressed head to toe in red.

Her heart rammed into her stomach.

Definitely, not a dream.

"The *Not-Cows*, the creature, the raven?" she mumbled. "They were real?"

He patted her shoulder gently. "Hallucinations are the worst." He shook his head. "It is the sap toxin. Seems it is not just a soporific, but has hallucinogenic properties as well."

A hazy shadow creased his blurry forehead

"And the hairless creature at the edge of the glade?"

Another wave of nausea washed over her.

The gnome didn't reply.

"But the *Not-Cows* weren't—" She rested her head in her

hands, to try to stop the spinning, and took a ragged breath.

"Their long hair protects them," he said. "The rodent in the grass had no—"

"Protection." Sally moaned. "And the raven didn't land in the grass."

"Raven?" He stopped what he was doing.

Sally nodded. "The white raven led me to you," she replied.

"There was no raven," he said calmly. He pressed the back of his hand on her forehead.

A hallucination?

"Thank goodness." She slumped against the wall. If she'd imagined the raven, then she'd imagined the terror in the sky. "Then the shadow creature was just a nightmare."

The gnome slipped his axe into a scabbard on his belt. "No, that was real," he said. "Well, as real as an invisible creature of shadow can be."

She had another impulse to retch.

This wasn't a dream. It was a nightmare. She just needed a hoard of ravenous garden gnomes to complete the horror.

"You will be all right." The gnome forced a smile. "I am just waiting for the bees to return, then I can fetch the herbs I require."

Sally shivered. "It's cold."

"That is the toxin spreading," he said.

"Can we have a fire?"

He shook his head. "Light attracts predators." He unrolled a scarlet cloak and wrapped it around her shoulders. "Much like your screaming."

The gnome continued the construction of the shelter, adding large bundles of sticks and large, odd-shaped leaves, then stood back, just beyond her focus, to examined his handiwork.

"All done. That should keep you out of harm's way while I'm gone." He turned to two bees by the shelter's doorway. "Let me know if you need me."

"You're leaving me?" She sat bolt upright. "Again?"

"Best not move or you will make it worse."

"What wors—?" Sally's vision blurred. The world twisted around her, colours bleeding together.

She yawned.

He placed both hands on her shoulders. His face now in clear focus. He looked directly into her eyes, eased her back onto the bed of moss, and pulled his cloak back over her.

"I will not be long. Our friends here are staying with you to keep guard." Two bees hovered over his shoulder. "They will alert me of any danger. The rest are scouting a safe passage through the forest."

He pulled out four long, slender plastic tubes - two yellow and two white - from a pocket deep inside his scarlet coat, and cracked a yellow tube. The shelter filled with a dim light. He tucked it in his belt and handed her the remaining three.

"Use them sparingly. I do not have many left. The yellow ones can last most of the night, but I cannot vouch for how long it will last here." He leaned his satchel against the wall next to her makeshift bed of moss. "Careful of the white ones. They are *flash sticks*." He paused at the entry. "And remember, nothing is as it seems here." He smiled. "I will be back as soon as I can."

"Alfred!" Sally's scream echoed inside the shelter. Glimpses of her nightmare haunted her. A cottage. Alfred's face - pale and clammy. The shadow creature. A grinning, red garden gnome. And herself - bound and gagged, unable to move. Unable to help.

The trill of cicadas serenaded her. Cool, crisp air blanketed the shelter. Rain tapped on the branches and twigs of the ceiling, creating a perfumed mix of the fresh aromas of wet soil, moss, and pine.

Sally's eyes snapped open. Pinpoints of pale light shone through the gaps between the woven-branch walls.

Specks of flickering golden light drifted in and out of the shelter. A straggler, with glowing bulbous abdomen, loitered and circled her head before meandering back through the ceiling to join its fellows.

Wood cracked outside the shelter wall. Sally's muscles tensed.

She slowly retrieved the light sticks the gnome had left her and rolled towards the shelter wall, trying to determine the origin of the noise.

A wave of nausea enveloped her as a pungent odour crept through the gaps. Her stomach heaved.

Leaves rustled.

Another snap.

Sally's heart pounded.

She slid each plastic bead along the cord of the friendship bracelet on her injured wrist, spelling out its message. Her heartbeat slowed.

Bees buzzed at the shelter opening. One scooted inside to join her. It zig-zagged above her head, relaying information.

"A Howler?" she whispered as she separated one of the

flash sticks and clutched it in her hand. She'd read about them in Olive's journal, one of The Books Protectors use to record their work.

There'd been an entry, in the early 1920s, mentioning a Howler in Humbug Scrub - not far away from her aunt's cottage.

She closed her eyes, trying to visualise the text. They were possible refugees from one the Otherworlds - Olive was never sure which - with a penchant for honey. Their stench would take days to leave the hive.

Sally opened her eyes and smiled. *They had a sweet tooth.*

She slid her hand into her pocket - trying to move as little as possible - where she'd stashed the Christmas toffees given to her by one of the regular Emergency patients, before her shift in children's ward this morning.

Or was it yesterday morning?

Her fingers curled around a small, hard toffee.

Her stomach grumbled.

She popped it in her mouth. It dissolved slowly, but did nothing to quell her hunger.

A snuffle, then a thud outside, made her jump. The wall beside her trembled.

The bees zoomed outside.

There was a short kerfuffle, and the snuffling retreated.

Sally lay still, listening to the din of the cicadas rising and falling. Wind whistled through the shelter wall. She shivered with each draft over her skin.

Her arm ached and her feet throbbed. She pulled the cloak around her shoulders, rolled onto her side, and jarred her elbow on a crooked branch sticking out from the wall.

She cried out. The scarlet cloak slid to the ground as she

sat bolt upright in pain. Deep, intense pain.

She cursed under her breath. The gnome's words replayed in her mind: *There's no telling what your screams attracted.*

She gritted her teeth and clutched her forearm tight, waiting for the pain to subside.

Her mind raced. If the bone was bruised, it could take months to heal. Time she didn't have. She needed to find Alfred. She needed more than her nursing skills this time. She needed magic.

Sally traced the scar the amulet had left at the base of her throat when it accepted her. It'd been beyond the ability for Aunt Enid's salve to cure, and magic didn't affect it; but the injury to her arm wasn't magical…

She slid her finger along the neckline of her dress and bit her lip. She hadn't needed a Focus last year when they fought the Darkness.

Perhaps her childhood injury provided an unexpected advantage? Perhaps the metal plate had served as a conduit?

Perhaps she didn't require an amulet either?

She closed her eyes, inhaled a long, slow breath, and focused on the training her aunts had drilled into her.

Step one: concentrate. That she could do; she'd done enough shifts in Emergency to know she could remain calm in chaos - that is, if garden gnomes weren't involved.

Step two: say the word. Words channelled the magic, reshaping it to the desired effect.

"Heal."

Nothing.

Sally growled. The words must be spoken *in Latin.* She really had to brush up on her Latin.

She rubbed her chin and tried to remember.

Cura? Sano? She smiled: "*Sano.*"

Heat grew inside her forearm. She grinned.

Something clicked. A bolt of pain seared under the skin.

Sally screamed.

🍪

Sally stretched out her arm, slowly testing the tendons and muscles of each finger, one at a time. So far, so good. She rotated her forearm.

Crunch.

Her arm recoiled back to her chest. Pain ricocheted along the bone.

"Shi—!" She bit her tongue as she felt the colour drain from her face.

Her head swam.

Her arm grew heavier with each throb of pain.

The magic had failed. She made a mental note to brush up on her Latin when she got home.

Her heart sank.

Home.

She winced as she lay back on the bed of soft moss, letting its rich earthy scent wrap around her like a comforting blanket, and inhaled deeply. The aroma filled her lungs.

Relax. Tensing her muscles would only intensify the pain, at least that's what she told her patients.

She scoffed. She didn't believe it, right now, either.

Another jolt of pain.

She flinched. The muscles in her arm tightened even more. She closed her eyes and growled in frustration, and pulled the cloak back over her shoulders.

Calm. You're a nurse. Remember your training.

She needed to immobilise the arm. She needed a sling.

Moonlight cast shadows where it couldn't penetrate the walls, making it too dim to see any details.

Sally sifted through the light sticks. What had the gnome said? The yellow ones burned slower; the white ones provided an intense flash of light? Right?

She selected a yellow one, narrowed her eyelids preparing for a possible flash, then snapped the plastic tube. With a satisfying crack, a gentle yellow glow filled the shelter.

She held it high and searched the shelter as she slipped the others into her skirt pocket.

Larger branches formed the shelter's frame between two trees. The walls were woven from smaller branches, with twigs and leaves stuffed into the larger crevices, allowing only a faint breeze through the side walls. In the opposite wall was an opening covered with a removable door. Heat radiated from three large stones half-buried in the soil.

A half-empty waterskin hung from a truncated branch next to her bed of moss. The gnome's satchel rested against the side wall, just out of arm's reach.

Sally opened the satchel. Surely, the gnome would have something to use as a sling?

Inside was a couple of glass jars wrapped in thin leather, a scroll case, a package wrapped in calico and smelling faintly of lavender and honey, a large bag of salt, and - tucked down the side - was a linen handkerchief embroidered with an 'R', not large enough to fashion a sling.

She unwrapped the handkerchief. Inside was a painted miniature of a woman and a child. A pang of guilt needled her. This was personal. An invasion of his privacy. She re-wrapped the miniature and tucked it down the side of the satchel next to the bag of salt, and replaced the satchel against the wall.

But she still needed a sling. She pulled one of the wrapped jars from the satchel, smashed it against one of the larger branches, and fished out a shard of glass. She poked it through her skirt as she tugged the fabric taut and ripped a wide strip from the bottom of her hem, then tentatively relaxed her arm into the makeshift sling, allowing it to take the full weight of her arm.

Exhaustion overwhelmed her.

Sally yawned and pulled the cloak tight around her. Her eyelids fluttered. She was exhausted. She wanted to lay down and sleep. But she couldn't; the gnome was gone, she had only two bees as sentries, there was something lurking outside, and—

Tap. Tap.

The entry cover jiggled.

Sally jumped. The light stick fell to the ground and rolled under the wall. The remaining light sticks slipped out of her pocket and rolled behind the satchel. She squinted trying to make out any shadows in the darkness.

Tap, tap, tap.

The cover rattled.

She reached for the light sticks.

Tap. Tap.

Crack.

The cover shifted. A gap appeared at its edges, and widened. A faint shaft of moonlight trickled through a gap.

Sally leaned further, stretching her fingers to reach the fallen light sticks, and lost her balance.

There was a rush of confusion.

The door cover toppled.

There was a flash of pale light, and a flurry of wings.

Flapping.

Cawing.

Screaming.

Pain.

A white raven settled on the satchel. It glowed in the moonlight.

Don't trust everything you see. Her aunt's warning whirled in her head.

She shifted uneasily and adjusted the sling as she eyed the bird. It seemed friendly. And it had guided her to the safety of the forest. And helped her find the gnome, when it could've left her to the shadow creature. And the bees would've warned her if it wasn't friendly.

The bird wavered in and out of focus as she rose slowly, leaning on the wall to keep her balance.

"Knock next time."

It cocked its head and stared at her with piercing pink eyes.

Muscles rippled under its feathers as it pecked at the cords of the satchel. A croaking purr rumbled in its throat. It pecked at a stray leaf poking through the wall.

Sally dropped onto the moss bed and flicked hair out of her face.

"Okay, but announce yourself, then."

Its neck snaked behind the satchel and retrieved one of the light sticks.

"Thank you." She reached out her hand, then hesitated. It was a wild creature, after all. She let her hand fall to her knee. "I owe you one."

Its hackles trembled as it cawed - the last, drawn-out note dropping in pitch, as if in agreement.

"I don't understand."

It cawed again.

"Alfred?" Sally shook her head. The raven had said his name. Impossible. It was the toxin. A hallucination. Her subconscious reminding her of her reason for travelling to this place. But it was right. Alfred needed her help.

It hopped onto the ground and pecked at some coloured stones half-buried in the dirt beside the satchel.

"Have you seen a tall man? Dark hair. Fancy waistcoat?" she asked.

It tilted its head.

Of course not. The chances would be remote. She needed something it may have seen, something from this world.

The image of a cottage flashed in her mind. Her dream.

"Do you know of a cottage?"

It didn't reply.

"Is there—?" A wave of nausea swept over her. She gripped the edge of the bed. Soft moss squished between her fingers. "Do you want me to do something?" she asked.

Its head twitched.

"Is there something you want…?" A shiver tracked over her skin. She swallowed. "Want me to do?"

It stared directly into her eyes.

Her head thumped.

Its croak was a gentle croon.

"I—" Her vision blurred. "Are you… hungry?" She reached for the satchel.

The bird snapped at her, its growl muffled.

"I don't think I can—" Her head whirled. She held her

sling tight and lowered herself back onto the bed. "You're right." Moving would speed up the toxin's effects.

The raven stretched out its wings and hopped onto the bed beside her.

The edges of her vision blurred. The toxin's effect was getter stronger. She closed her eyes, clutched the light stick, and sank her fingers into the moss bed, trying to ground herself.

Wind buffeted the roof. Shadows flickered across the floor and coalesced into a single form looming over her.

chapter seven

The walls shuddered. The shadow dissolved, replaced by another, shorter silhouette, half its height.

Sally's heart pounded. Her fingers burned. She thrust the light stick into the air, squeezed her eyes shut, and cracked it.

A brilliant burst of white light seared through her eyelids and engulfed the intruder.

"Death's head on a mopstick!"

She knew that voice. She waited for the light to fade, then opened her eyes.

"Are you all right," asked the gnome asked. A guard of bees buzzed at his shoulder.

The wind howled around the shelter, tousling his yellow hair as it whipped through the doorway.

She nodded.

He leaned two sticks - each as thick as his thumbs - against the shelter wall as he entered. A flank of bees followed him; the other half remained outside and took up watch.

A leather pouch dropped onto the bed beside her.

"This should do the trick. The toxin is very much like—"

His gaze flicked over the shelter. "Where are your bees?" A second pouch landed, with a squelch, next to her.

She scanned the shelter. They were gone. And so was the raven.

"You scared away the raven." Sally sat up slowly.

"Raven?" He frowned.

"It was just here," she replied. "I think it wanted me to go to the cottage."

"There was no raven." He leaned his axe against the wall. Worry lines etched his forehead. "What cottage?"

He pulled up Sally's eyelids one at a time, and examined her eyes. "Hmm… Perhaps the hallucinogen in the toxin was stronger than I thought."

Sally sighed with relief. "Then the shadow creature was a hallucination?"

"No," he replied. "That was real."

He pressed his hand against her forehead.

"You are burning up. I've been gone too long." He growled. "The bees should have informed me."

The world wavered. Sally fell back onto the bed.

He hummed as he rummaged through his satchel, paused, and glanced at Sally out of the corner of his eye. He scooped up the pouches from the bed and continued his melancholy, and oddly comforting, tune.

Sally's muscles relaxed. She closed her eyes, letting the tune roll over her like a blanket.

Noises filtered in from outside the shelter: the soft scuff of moving debris, scraping of rocks, snapping of sticks, and the chink of striking stones. All the time, he hummed the lilting tune.

Sally cradled her injured arm and rolled onto her left side.

The gnome crouched over a mound of small twigs. A short wall of rocks and branches had been raised on the other side of him.

Sparks spewed from his flint. One caught a tuft of dry leaves. A faint glow winked in the darkness. He cupped his hand and blew gently. It flickered and grew until a small flame licked the twigs.

Sally breathed slowly, forcing her brain to form each word. "Thought fire attracted predators?"

"Your need is greater."

He rocked back onto his haunches, attached the shorter of the two sticks he'd brought back with him, to the other, and drove it into the ground near the fire, then hooked a ceramic kettle onto the horizontal one.

His face was lit by the growing fire, his eyes calm and kind. A smile twitched over his lips. He brushed the soil off his hands before he opened one of the pouches, removed bits of moss and leaves, then pulled a few petals from a small blue flower and dropped them into the teapot, and hummed as he stirred the brew.

Once the brew bubbled, he opened the second pouch and squeezed a pink, vile-smelling sludge into the pot. A puff of orange steam twisted into the air.

The vapour wafted into the shelter. Sally cringed. This was the antidote for the toxin? She wrinkled her nose. It smelled like a morgue during a heatwave.

"Am I…" she croaked, each word barely a whisper as they emerged, "supposed… t—" She gulped as the words scratched her dry throat. "Drink that?"

Her stomach curdled. She hoped he knew what he was doing.

She closed her eyes and listened to crackling fire and the sputtering liquid hiss when it hit the flames. Exhaustion tugged at her consciousness, pulling her down. Her limbs grew heavier. Her muscles relaxed back into the moss she lay on, and her breathing slowed in time with the gnome's deep voice. Was it a lullaby, to aid rest, or a prayer pleading to save her, or a eulogy for the dying?

She shivered, struggling to keep her eyes open. Sweat dripped down her temple. She tried to lift her hand to wipe her forehead. It refused to move.

She caught her breath, and tried to swing her legs off the bed.

No response.

Red! The scream echoed through her head, but there was no sound.

The humming stopped. Gentle hands lifted her head.

A foul stench of rotting leaves and, what smelled like rancid meat and rotten egg. She grimaced, but had no strength to pull away.

Don't make me drink that. She forced open her eyes.

The gnome had a glass jar in his hand. Dark chunks swirled in the shimmering pink liquid.

He pressed the jar to her lips. She gagged.

"You need to drink this." The gnome's voice was muffled, deeper than usual.

He tilted it slowly. Warm glass touched her lips. Thick, hot liquid trickled into her mouth and down her throat. A sour, fermented taste - she spluttered - with a cheesy-vinegar aftertaste.

The liquid slowed. A warm breath brushed her ear.

"Please." His hand trembled. "You *must* drink it."

Again, the liquid filled her mouth. Her stomach churned. She swallowed.

Needles of bright moonlight pierced the gaps between the woven branches of the shelter's roof. Wood creaked in the wind; a high-pitched squeaking as it complained. Flakes of bark drifted to the ground in the shafts of moonlight.

Outside, leaves rustled in the forest canopy, cicadas trilled their serenade, and a night bird churred softly as it relocated to another tree.

There was a faint croak in the distance.

Sally sucked in a sharp breath. Was it the raven? Or was she hallucinating again?

A snuffle directed her attention to the open shelter entrance.

The gnome leaned against the door frame with his back to her, his elbow hooked around the shaft of the axe. His shoulders rose and fell with each breath.

His long shadow flickered across the shelter floor, dancing with the dying flames of the campfire. Outside, embers glowed red, lifted up into the air, and drifted towards the shelter, winking out before they reached the sleeping gnome. An occasional renegade singed his hair.

Sally tilted her head; he didn't look so scary now he was flesh and blood. How had she been so scared of a ceramic garden ornament? Perhaps that's why the hordes of garden gnomes no longer filled her nightmares? Instead, gingerbread fairies invaded her dreams, forcing themselves down her throat.

She slipped the remaining two light sticks into her sling,

rose slowly, and crept across the shelter pausing momentarily to let the heat radiating from the stones in the ground warm her, before turning sideways to edge past the gnome.

Swish.

An axe barred her way.

"Where do you think you are going?" The gnome's voice was calm, just like when her aunt scolded her. "It is not safe out there."

He glared at her from the corner of his eye.

"I heard a noise," she replied. *Not a lie.*

"The forest is full of noises." He swung his axe onto his shoulder. "You need to be more specific."

A bird croaked in the trees above them. Sally shifted uneasily. The scarlet cloak slipped off one shoulder.

"Just an owl." He stretched his shoulders. "Most likely a Nightjar."

"I have to find Alfred. I've wasted too much time. He could be injured. We need to—"

"You are not going anywhere in the dark. Besides." Red shook his head. "You need more rest. The toxin will not be out of your system before morning." He offered her the half-empty waterskin that had been hanging in the shelter. "Here, drink this."

She eyed it, hoping it wasn't another of his foul-tasting concoctions.

"It is just water." He wiggled the waterskin. "You have my word."

"But it's the last of the water," she said.

"I was told nurses make bad patients," he replied. "You need it more than I. You need to keep hydrated." He shoved it into her hand.

He sat on one of the upturned stumps and prodded the fire. A rush of embers flew into the air. A wave of heat washed over her.

Wind tousled the leaves. Moonlight filtered down through breaks in the canopy and danced across the forest floor. A faint shadow flitted in the darkness.

A slow cawing croak trickled through the trees, dropping at the end. A high-pitched shriek followed.

"Tell me you heard that?" she whispered.

"Sounded like another owl."

A streak of white glinted in the deep shadows.

"There's something out there," Sally whispered.

"There usually is," he replied.

"I'm serious." She hugged her arm and turned towards the noise.

The gnome peered into the forest.

"I cannot see anything." He rested his hand gently on her shoulder. "The toxin's hallucinogenic effects can linger for a while."

Deeper in the forest, another creature screeched.

Sally wobbled.

"Sit down." The gnome pushed a wood stump towards her. "You are still recovering."

She slumped onto the hard stump.

He draped his cloak back over her shoulders.

"How is the arm?" he asked. "I am surprised you have not magicked a cure yet."

"I…" She pulled at a loose thread on the edge of the sling. "I tried. But, I can't." She tugged the cloak over the sling. "I don't have my amulet." She rubbed the raised scar at the base of her neck, where Olive's amulet had branded her when it claimed her. "No amulet; no magic."

"It is the curse of the Otherworlds, for a Traveller, and likely why Protectors do not venture through portals," he replied. "Many will not allow the passage of metal."

She clutched her arm in the sling. He didn't need to know about the metal plate in her arm, yet.

"Though you have focused the *Aether* without a conduit in the past."

"But something is still needed to channel it." Sally replied.

"Aether, yes." He looked her directly in the eye. "There are other ways to access *magick*."

"Other ways?" Her stomach fluttered.

"*Wild Magick*,"

"*Wild*—?" Sally shook her head.

"It has been done before."

"But…" She'd read about it in Olive's Book. Under no circumstances was it to be used. Too unpredictable. Uncontrollable. Dangerous. "But it's forbidden for a Protector to use *Wild Magick*."

"It is also forbidden for your kind to travel to Otherworlds. Yet, here we are."

"To save a friend."

"Yes." The gnome's lips curled at the corner. "T*o save a friend.*"

"No." Sally tucked the frayed edges into the sling. "I can't." She stared into the dying flames of the campfire. "Not even for a friend," she whispered. She'd have to find another way.

The gnome retrieved his axe. The reflection of dying flames licked the metal and highlighted the decorative inlays along the hilt.

Metal. How was it he could bring metal through the portal, and she couldn't?

"How did you bring your axe through the portal?" she asked.

"I am a Traveller." He leaned on the axe as if no further explanation was required.

Sally frowned. Why was he so secretive?

"I don't understand." She leaned in closer. "Pretend I'm new to the 'Protector-Otherworlds' thing."

He rested the axe across his knees. "A ceramic garden gnome when through the portal. I changed back into a creature of bone and blood when I touched Otherworlds soil."

"That's medically impossible!" The human body won't—." Her cheeks flushed. He wasn't human. "I mean…"

Her mind raced with questions. She took a sip from the waterskin.

"Do all Travellers become garden gnomes?" she asked. "Ceramic, I mean?"

"Not all Travellers show their true self in your world," he replied. "It is an illusion. *Magick.* We were sent to assist the Protectors, so transformed into something less intimidating to mortals. You are a skittish lot." The corner of his mouth twitched. "There are Protectors on all the worlds. Not just Earth. We go where we are needed."

"Surely, not all garden gnomes are Travellers?" she scoffed.

He shook his head, but proffered no further information.

She screamed internally with frustration. Why was he making it so hard? It was like the games the kids played with her in the Children's Ward. She'd have to take a different approach.

Wait, 'back'?

"You're from an Otherworld?"

He nodded.

She remembered the miniature in his satchel. He had a family. Or did, once. Guilt gnawed her gut. She tugged the cloak tighter to give her courage to ask the question.

"Were you always a garden gnome?"

He raised an eyebrow. "I am… We are Guardians to the Protectors."

"I mean, how long have you been on Earth?"

He chased an errant ember around the edge of the firepit. "I became a Guardian one hundred and eighty-seven years and twelve days ago.

He stared at the firepit, avoiding her gaze.

Sally's heart broke. She had so many questions: *Why did you leave your family? Do you miss your home?* But the growing guilt of invading his privacy stayed her tongue.

Finally, she asked: "Are all your people Guardians?"

He straightened his shoulders. "We call ourselves the *G'nonri*." His rich, deep voice wrapped around the 'o' and rolled the 'r'. "And no, not all of us are Guardians," he replied.

"Then there are other Travellers on Earth?" she asked.

"Yes."

"So, they can travel between worlds whenever they want?" She wondered if her aunts knew.

"No, not all those from Otherworlds are Travellers. There are sightseers, and many refugees, though not all Protectors recognise that status. And there are those who just want a less complicated world without *magick*." He chuckled softly. "It is complicated. Many arrive via existing portals."

"Like the fairy doors in town?" she asked.

"Yes. Did you learn that from *The Books*?"

"There's a note about them in Olive's Book." She frowned. "You've never read them?"

"They are private. For Protectors only." He looked directly in her eyes as if to make a point. "It would break a trust."

He knew. She swallowed.

"Do my aunts know about Travellers?" she said.

A fleeting smile tugged at the corner of his lips. "You should ask your Aunt Agnes about that one day."

Sally's ears pricked. *Agnes?*

His smile broadened. "Protectors have many secrets. More secrets than me."

Sally eyed him. "Still doesn't answer my question."

He leaned back and rested his hands on his thighs. "Like I said: It is comp—"

A screech echoed in the forest canopy.

Sally jumped.

The gnome snatched up his axe, and scanned the trees as he rose slowly to his feet.

"That wasn't an owl," she whispered.

"No, it was not." He searched the encroaching darkness; the moon had set and the fire had burned down to coals. allowing the shadows to envelope them.

"Best you take cover." He motioned for her to return to the shelter. He scattered the glowing coals, and kicked dirt over the remainders of the fire.

Wood creaked as he wiggled the door cover into place.

His axed thudded on the outside of the wall. He hummed quietly - the same soft lilting tune, that made Sally feel she was swinging slowing in a warm breeze. Her limbs grew heavy. She tugged the cape over her shoulders, lay down, and closed her eyes.

The shelter smelled of pine and warm soil.

Sally's stomach grumbled. She hadn't eaten since yesterday morning, or at least it was yesterday back home. Who knew long it's been? The gnome said she'd slept one day, but could she really trust him?

She sat up on the bed; the earthy smell of moss followed her.

Sweat beaded on her forehead. The nightmares were getting more vivid the deeper they delved into the forest. Visions of gingerbread fae lingered - clamouring over her, in place of garden gnomes - and ravens leading her towards a bright light, which engulfed her as she woke.

And the strange cottage… There was always the cottage, this time surrounded by sparkling silver pine trees.

The patter of footsteps scuttled across the roof. A shadow moved across the lower half of the door. The gnome had stood guard all night.

Daylight leaked through the gaps between the woven branches of the roof.

She'd slept too long.

Sally tested her feet on the ground, pleasantly surprised there was no pain.

A burst of warmth bathed her legs as she launched herself over the heating stones in the ground. She flung the door cover aside.

A flutter of wings lifted from the roof.

The gnome's cloak slipped from her shoulder. He caught it with his axe, and shifted to one side.

A wall of cold air greeted her.

Sally cursed under her breath.

"Not a morning person, I see." He chuckled as he smoothed branch nubs off a long, straight branch taller than him, with his knife.

She glared at him.

"Sorry I have no caffeine to ease you into the day."

"Why did you let me sleep in?" she hissed. "Alfred has been out all night in this chill. *Alone*. I have to find him."

"I have sent the bees to look for his tracks," he replied. He handed her the branch. "This is for you." He nodded in the direction of her bandaged feet. "To help you walk."

Sally dusted off her skirt.

She glanced at the cold firepit. "No fire today?" She'd hoped there might be something for breakfast. Her stomach gurgled loudly, betraying her thoughts.

The gnome shood his head. "It is not safe to—"

"Eat anything." She huffed. "Yes, I remember." Her stomach tightened in protest.

"I thought that only meant if it was offered to you by strange Fac. Surely, we could source our own?"

"And how will you know if it is poisonous? Remember the grass?"

Sally winced and nodded.

"I am not familiar with the life forms on this world," he said.

She licked her dry lips.

He sat on one of the logs by the firepit, removed the calico package from his satchel, and offered her half of a small, dense lavender and honey bun. She bit into it. It was hard as rock.

"Here." He picked up a small jar from under a string of curled, funnel-like leaves hanging from the corner of the shelter. Water dripped slowly from the bottom leaf onto the ground where the jar had sat. "It helps if you soak it in water."

She sniffed the water dubiously. "Is it safe?"

He poured some into his cupped palm and sipped it.

"Yes." He handed her the jar.

She examined the jar in her hand, dipped the bun in the water and swallowed a large mouthful. "Aren't you having any?"

He retrieved an empty jar from the top of the rough firewall and shook it.

"I have already eaten." He slung his satchel over his shoulder, and picked up his axe. "Best relieve yourself before we leave." He strode towards a stand of bushes behind the shelter.

Sally snorted.

He halted. "What?"

"I'm not ten," she replied.

The gnome smiled. "Then do not complain if we do not have time later."

Sally stifled a grin.

"Yes, mum," she mumbled under her breath.

"And put the cloak back on. You will need it." His voice trailed as he sank behind the undergrowth.

Sally guzzled down the rainwater, retrieved the scarlet

cloak and circled behind the shelter and scanned the ground for a suitable spot to—

A glint of light in the grass behind the shelter caught her eye. She examined it closer: a thin transparent wing, partially attached to a fuzzy, mangled body, with hints of black and yellow stripes.

The cloak tumbled to the ground beside her.

"Red?" The words caught in her throat.

She pinched one of the surviving wings between her fingers and held it up to the light. A bee wing.

She brushed aside the leaf litter. Two more wings. No wonder she hadn't seen her guardians all night.

Sally cradled them in her hand and returned to the firepit, and called in a louder voice: "Red?"

"Just a minute," replied his gruff voice.

She sat on the closest stump.

Footsteps crunched on the fallen leaves behind her - each step sounding like crunching insects.

"What is it?" He picked up the cloak and shook of the leaves.

Sally held out her hand to show him the bees' remains.

"Death's head on a mopstick." He slumped onto the stump next to her. "I wondered where the scoundrels had gotten to." He handed her the cloak and pulled a convex lens from a pocket and examined them closely. "Looks like the work of an avian."

"The owl?" she asked.

"Perhaps."

A flank of bees swooped out of the trees. The gnome closed his hand over the wing remnants and held it behind his back.

The bees buzzed around his head.

"They have found some tracks." He nodded. "And human shoe prints."

Sally addressed the bees: "Thank you," she said. "Show me."

The bees flew into the trees.

The gnome dug a small hole in the dirt with his index finger, whispered under his breath as he buried the wings, and led Sally deeper into the forest, after the bees.

chapter eight

With each step, pain burrowed into the soles of Sally's feet. She regretted discarding her sandshoes in the glade. The forest floor was littered with debris: fallen sticks, low-lying bracken, rocks and - worst of all - a particularly nasty form of prickly nettle.

She leaned on the walking staff, to transfer some weight off her feet and clenched her toes, trying to minimise contact with the ground.

"Keep up." The gnome strode ahead, guided by the bees, in his hard-soled, leather boots, seemingly oblivious to her pain.

Another broken twig dug into her instep, grazing the skin. Sharp pain sliced across the soles of her feet.

Sally winced, and halted.

The bees paused and hovered ahead of them. One circled back to join her.

The gnome stopped, hefted his axe and scanned the trees around them.

"Did you see something?" he asked.

She shook her head.

"I just need a minute." She leaned against a nearby tree

and examined her foot: mostly superficial grazes and a few small lacerations, but the twig had buried deeper than she'd expected. Beads of blood formed at the site of the injury.

The gnome extracted a crisp, linen handkerchief from a coat pocket and handed it to her.

The bees hovered by his shoulder. He examined her foot as she wiped it clean.

"That needs wrapping." He lowered his axe and rummaged through his satchel, and removed a small, round glass pot.

"I am a nurse, remember." She was used to treating others, not being a patient. "I can do it."

"Very well." He handed her the jar. "I have some bandages." He delved back into the satchel.

Sally removed the lid, scooped out a creamy salve, and smeared a line along the deep graze. The aroma of lavender, witch hazel, tea tree and beeswax filled her nostrils. It was cool - she caught her breath - and stung slightly.

She took the bandages from the gnome, and wrapped her feet. If she layered them enough, they'd protect her soles from further injury.

Sharp bark dug into her hip through her thin cotton dress. She listed to one side, still feeling the aftereffects of the toxin, and caught herself, making sure not to let the salve-slathered sole touch the ground.

"Let me do it." The gnome held out his hand and waited. "I may not be a medic, but I do have battlefield training."

The bees buzzed in agreement.

Sally struggled to keep her balance. Aunt Enid told her to trust him, and she had no other choice; the wounds needed dressing and she doubted she could continue the search for

Alfred with her feet as they were.

She nodded, handed him the bandages, and watched closely, ready to offer instructions as needed. He was surprisingly gentle; he wrapped the foot tightly - but not too tight - then tied moss to the bottom of the bandages with leather cord removed from his remaining bracer.

"To keep the bandages clean," he said.

Sally tested her weight on one foot. The bandages held tight, cushioning and distributing the pressure, so she could barely feel the pain. It would still be slow going.

The bees turned in unison and continued forward, guiding them onward.

Sally trudged on, following the gnome as he tracked Alfred's footprints through the forest, stopping occasionally to converse with the bees and to check her progress.

Around them, branches creaked and leaves rustled. Creatures whistled and squawked as they flew overhead, and the occasional animal skittered through bushes as they approached.

A flurry of movement in the undergrowth ahead halted the party.

A loud shriek followed. A ripple of excited chittering grew closer, bringing with it a flutter of wings increasing in pitch as the sound moved closer. Up ahead, flickering silvery lights wove between the tree trunks edging ever closer.

A single bee darted out of the vegetation and sped towards her companions. The bees fussed and retreated to join the gnome.

He hefted his weapon and took a few steps forward.

The lights turned in their direction.

Sally halted, and watched as they flitted through the forest revealing the vibrant colours of the trees and flowers as they passed.

Her hand brushed a velvety, petal of a large teal-blue flower with purple-tipped petals as large as her hand. The flower opened. Its tufted red stamens trembled as it turned to face her. A mesmerising perfume, of honey, and maple syrup, and roses, overwhelmed her.

It sang to her; a clear, tinkling harmony vibrated her eardrum inducing a pleasing sensation, like cool water bathing her skin on a scorching summer day.

"Get down." The gnome shoved Sally towards the nearest tree and dove behind the closest bush.

The bees darted past her, buzzing a warning and pushing her back into the cover of a tree hollow, out of sight.

The bees went silent.

Sally peeked through the low-lying branches, ignoring the twigs that scratched her.

The gnome wasn't visible.

The lights moved faster as they drew closer. They resembled dragonflies, each with a body almost a metre long and wing spans twice as wide. Their iridescent, segmented wings shimmered in the pulsing illumination of their glowing abdomens.

A long, needle-sharp proboscis extended and pierced the centres of the flowers. The petals trembled, their song now a high-pitched scream like shattering glass.

Sally held her breath as the monstrous insectoids rammed their proboscises deeper into the flowers' flesh. The plump petals convulsed and shrivelled slowly as they guzzled, their vibrant colours fading with each gulp.

The insects peeled away, one at a time, until only one remained, gorging itself on a flower less than a metre away from Sally's hiding place.

Its abdomen glowed brighter with each gulp.

Sally's hands trembled. She had to stop it. She stepped forward.

The bush next to her twitched. A black glove pushed through the branches and clasped her arm, holding her back.

"Best to avoid the local wildlife," he whispered.

The flower's scream burrowed into her head. She clenched her teeth, feeling every pulse of its pain. And she could do nothing. She wanted to call out, to chase the insect away. Instead, she bit her tongue, stayed by the gnome's hand.

The flower shuddered as the insectoid extracted its feeding tube. With a final shriek, it collapsed and crumpled to the ground. The insectoid hovered, as if sensing them, then darted off after the others.

"They have gone." The gnome pushed a branch aside and emerged from his cover, his black eyes lined with concern. "Protector?"

The bees exited the hollow, circled them, and continued further into the forest.

The gnome offered Sally a hand.

She waved him away. "I can do it myself, thank you."

She squirmed out of the tree, tugging her snagged skirt free from a twig, and stared at the flower.

"I could've saved it," she whispered.

"And you would have died doing so," he replied.

Sally shook her head. "You would've stopped them."

The gnome frowned. "There was no guarantee of that. I

am but one, separated from my company. I do not know this world. They could be like wasps; kill one and more come." He dusted his red cap off on his sleeve and replaced it on his head. "And we do not want to attract attention to ourselves."

He glanced after the bees. "Time to go."

They continued on in silence; the gnome checking tracks, and the bees buzzing instructions, until they reached a small clearing. Sunlight shone through a break in the canopy where the trees thinned. A vague track became visible.

The gnome halted and knelt to examine the ground. He mumbled something to the bees. They parted into two groups and drifted along the tree line in opposite directions.

"Are you sure he went this way?" Sally glanced over his shoulder.

He pointed at the indentations in the soft, wet soil. There were two sets of tracks; the shoe prints they'd been following, and a set of paw prints crossing over them, with a wide pad and four toes and a ghost-like impression of a fifth toe to the side.

"He is being followed." The gnome rose. "Looks like a Howler."

"I have to find Alfred." Sally followed the footprints. "Before it catches up with him."

A few steps further and both sets of prints blurred.

"Wait," hissed the gnome. "I have sent the bees to—"

She ignored him and strode towards the clearing.

He grasped her arm and pointed into the clearing. A faint shadow lingered over the ground.

"Listen," he hissed.

A faint peal of bells tinkled above them.

Sally's heart pounded. She retreated back under cover. The gnome pulled her into the shadows and behind a stand of trees at the edge of the clearing.

Sally peeked around the trunk. The sunlight was fading making the creature's shadow harder to see. Another tinkle of bells. She pressed her back against the tree.

"The shadow creature?" she whispered.

"It must have followed us." He released her arm.

"How did you know?"

"The blurred tracks in the clearing," he replied. "They were running. That is never a good sign." He scanned the sky. "I have sent the bees to find the tracks on the other side. If you trusted me to do my job, then the creature would not know we're here."

A thought haunted her mind; she tugged her cloak tight, refusing to believe it. "What if there aren't any more tracks?"

The gnome replied in a calm voice, but avoided eye contact. "The bees will find them."

They remained still, waiting for the shadow to move and the bells to fade.

Sally's stomach growled. Her arm ached and her feet throbbed; both in time with her thumping heart.

Her hand prickled with heat. She slipped it into her pocket and curled her fingers around the remaining toffee. She hesitated. She'd eaten breakfast; Alfred would need it more.

She was relieved when the bees returned and informed them of tracks on the far side of the clearing.

They followed their guides until the gnome picked up the tracks on the other side. Two sets: human shoe prints and the four-toed creature, walking side-by-side.

A guard of bees flanked Sally and the gnome on either side, as they continued through the forest.

Purple and yellow sky peeked through the gaps in the treetops. The forest was getting dark and they still hadn't found Alfred.

Sally's feet complained as small twigs and leaves worked their way under the edge of the bandages. She tied to hide her limp from the gnome; she knew he'd force her to rest.

He slowed to let her catch up. "Problem?"

She hesitated, leaning on her walking staff to take the weight of her feet. "No." Her fingertips tingled. "Yes." She flexed them, trying to still them. "The sun is going down and we haven't found anything but tracks. He could be—"

Bees hovered by the gnome's head. He nodded and eyed the glimpses of sky between the trees.

"It is getting late. We should rest."

A chill breeze caught the edge of her cloak. With it, came the faint fetid stench of rotten eggs. She screwed up her nose.

The gnome inhaled deeply. "Come on."

He strode through a line of bushes and disappeared.

"Wait for me." Sally hobbled after him.

The stench grew stronger. There were now hints of sulphides and rotting vegetation, accompanied by the sounds of splashing water and sucking mud.

A few steps beyond the bushes, she barrelled into the gnome.

"Death's head on a mopstick!" He jumped back to stop falling forward, and landed in a bush.

The light sticks slipped out of Sally's sling, plopped onto the ground, and sank slowly. She grabbed for them.

"Best not." He pointed to a faint ripple in the water a couple of metres to their right.

"You've got more, right?" she asked as they disappeared from view.

"One flash stick only." He shook slimy water off his boot and tested the ground around them. "Swamp," he growled. He surveyed the area. "Bloody big one, too."

Tree trunks pierced the still surface of the swamp as far as the eye could see. Fading sunlight broke through the thinning canopy above, casting long shadows over the water's rainbow-coloured surface.

"The colours. It's…" *Wow.* Sally inhaled a breath. She gagged and covered her nose with her arm.

"Did you see?" Her hand fumbled in the gnome's direction to get his attention.

"Yes, yes." He tested the ground a few metres to their left, and shook his head.

"It's beautiful."

"The polychromatic effect?" He searched along the edge of the water. "It is the rotting vegetation." He stared at the swamp and rubbed the back of his neck. "There are no more tracks."

A light flickered in the shadows just beyond a fallen tree. A white shape rose above it. It turned to face Sally, spread its wings, and flew away from them, further into the swamp and settled on a fallen tree.

Her heart skipped. "The raven's back to show us the way."

He shook his head.

Sally frowned "No, I saw—"

"*Ghost Lights*." He pointed to a glowing pale-blue light bobbing in the distance.

Her shoulders slumped. She'd been so certain…

"If there were no more tracks, then Alfred must've crossed the swamp." She pointed to where the raven had landed.

"See how strong the colours are on the surface?" he asked. "The effect becomes stronger, the longer the water remains undisturbed."

The bees swarmed in front of Sally, forming a line between her and the swamp. Their warning boomed through her head.

She slid to the ground with a thud. Her eyes stung. The swamp's stench clung to the back of her throat. She wiped away tears with the back of her hand.

A strong hand pulled her to her feet. "Can you smell that?"

The wind had shifted, now coming from their right and not across the swamp.

"Of course." Sally spluttered. "That's the problem."

"No," He turned to face the narrow path formed by the natural outcrop of rock they stood on. "That."

Sally reluctantly sniffed the air. "Old mouldy socks?"

"Close enough." The gnome grinned. "That is a Howler." He strode along the path, into the breeze. "I recognised those tracks." "Keep up."

chapter nine

Cicadas trilled from every corner of the forest. The ripe smell of old socks and fresh manure made Sally's eyes water. She screwed up her nose. The gnome sniffed the air, and turned towards the smell.

The bees darted ahead.

"This way." He edged through a thicket of bushes. "Watch out."

"Why are we tracking a Howler?" She rubbed her hand. "I thought you said we should avoid the local wildlife?"

"If they are local, they will know the lie of the land."

"*If* they're local?"

"It is the best option we have, right now. Howlers are like rats; they are on almost every world." He sidestepped a tree trunk. "They may help us to track his scent."

"You can't track him?" she asked.

He scoffed. "My olfactory senses are not that good, but thank you for the compliment."

She fingered the fragment of red silk in her dress pocket.

"Would this work?" She held it up. "I think it's from his waistcoat."

He nodded. "Perfect."

The stench rolled over them. It reeked of death. Sally gagged and covered her nose.

The gnome halted and raised his arm to bar the way.

At his feet was a mound of crumpled grey jacket. Long rents ripped through the material revealing hints of red silk lining. She glanced at the remnant from her pocket. The lining was an exact match.

Her heart sank.

"Is that…?" She sucked in a sharp breath. "Alfred?" Her voice cracked.

"Wait here," he whispered in a deep voice.

Sally picked up the shredded jacket. One of the inside pockets had been wrenched away from the lining and hung by a couple of threads; possibly the result of his lockpicks being torn out by the portal.

She hugged it close.

A few metres away, the gnome stood over the carcass of a dog-like creature with short, smooth greyish hair and darker stripes along the body. Large gashes ran along its neck.

"Is that a Howler?" she asked.

He nodded.

"Looks like it has been dead less than two days." He knelt beside the corpse, apparently oblivious to the stench - so much for his 'superior olfactory senses'- and inserted a stick into one of the puncture marks in its neck.

"And Alfred?"

Her fingers buzzed. The scratches on her arms felt as if they were on fire.

If the Howler was… then, Alfred…

Her hands dug into the jacket. She swallowed.

Then Alfred was probably…

Saying the words out loud would make it real. She clutched the jacket tighter.

"Protector?"

The din of the cicadas dulled.

Yellow and black smudges circled her head, buzzing in her ears. She waved them away.

The gnome's voice faded.

Her heart raced and her chest felt like it would implode. She gasped for breath.

Alfred was...

Her fingertips burned.

And the world turned.

The smell of singed wool snapped her attention back to the corpse at their feet.

Sally blinked. She was on her knees. Someone was talking.

"Breathe." A deep voice whispered in her ear. "Just breathe." The voice was clearer now. Familiar. "I found more tracks."

The gnome.

She shook her head, to steady the world. A hint of ozone lingered.

"Human adult-sized prints, leading away."

His hand touched her shoulder.

"He's not dead." He stared into her eyes. *Black. Pupilless.* She couldn't tell if he was lying.

He held out his hand to help her up.

Sally picked up the walking staff he'd made her, pushed herself to her feet, and dusted off her skirt, Alfred's jacket still grasped tight to her chest.

His gaze flicked away from her feet. He eyed the jacket

in her hands as she ran her fingers along the jacket's lapel.

"Let me keep this safe." He inspected it briefly, rolled it up, and slipped it into his satchel.

Sally rubbed her temples. "You said there were tracks?"

The gnome nodded. "This way."

The bees turned and followed the tracks. Sally hobbled past him, after their guides. The gnome followed.

The last light of the suns had disappeared from view.

Sally was barely able to make out the outline of the gnome less than two metres in front of her, still humming the same wistful tune from the previous night. The bees flanked her, buzzing directions as she stepped warily in the low light, feeling her way.

Sally's feet dragged. She stifled a yawn.

A chill wind caught her hair. She shivered and stumbled over a root. The last remnants of the moss padding, tied to the soles of her feet, crumbled away. The leather cords holding it slackened and slipped down her foot. She kicked them off, and landed her foot on a sharp twig.

She moaned in pain.

The gnome slowed. "I can't see any more tracks."

"There has to be." She drew a long deep breath to centre her thoughts. A faint whiff of woodsmoke tickled her nose. They must be getting close to the edge of the forest - closer to the smoke she saw beyond the forest when she arrived. They had to keep moving. She had to find Alfred. "We can use one of the light sticks."

"We only have a flash stick left," he said. "The others are at the bottom of the swamp." He halted. "Besides, we do not want to—"

"To attract the local wildlife," she continued in a whisper. "I know."

"Exactly."

The bees buzzed in agreement.

In the distance, a meandering light glowed faintly.

"I *have* to find Alfred." She stumbled through bushes, feeling her way around a tree trunk. Its rough bark scraped her skin.

She edged past Red and walked on.

He sighed and followed. "We should rest."

"I can't," she hissed. "You must've smelled the smoke."

"I did."

"Perhaps we can find help?"

He grunted.

"Or not?" replied Sally.

Another rush of cold air curled around her calves and lifted her cloak. She pulled it tight.

"Where's there's smoke, there's fire. And where there's fire, there's…" Her teeth chattered. "There's heat. Alfred would've been freezing without his jacket. He'd have followed the smoke."

"Agreed."

"But we—" Sally blinked. Had he agreed with her?

"*I* need a rest." The gnome rested his axe against a tree trunk. "And those bandages need changing." He hummed as he rummaged in his satchel.

A drift of large fireflies floated nearby.

The gnome stopped humming.

The fireflies slowed and hovered. The gnome started humming again. They drifted closer.

He extracted a jar from his satchel, and crept towards them.

They wove between the tree trunks, gravitating closer.

The gnome remained motionless until they were on top of him. In less than a heartbeat, he scooped up one of the stragglers and snapped the lid on the jar. The insect twisted in the close confines of the jar. Its flickering golden light glinted in the gnome's eyes and illuminated his grin.

Sally's feet itched. She leaned against a trunk and picked at the bandages on her feet.

He placed the jar next to her. "Let me do it."

He gently pushed her hand aside and peeled off the layers of cloth, reapplied fresh salve to the almost healed wounds, and replaced them with fresh bandages from his satchel - all the while, humming as he worked.

"Are you some sort of Mary Poppins with a bottomless carpet bag?"

"I have my secrets," he replied.

His melancholy tune slowed; her heartbeat slowing with it.

Sally yawned.

"I had the same nightmare again," she mumbled "That's three nights in a row. Is that an omen?"

"Probably the toxin," he replied.

She slumped back against the tree.

He continued to hum.

Her eyelids fluttered as she covered another yawn.

"Is there a sedative in that salve?" she asked.

A smile flickered over his face.

"Hang on." She frowned. "That tune. It's a lullaby, isn't it?"

He grinned, still humming.

"Stop it." Another yawn. "Is it… You have…" She slid down the trunk. "*Magick?*"

He cradled her head in his arms.

"No *magick,*" she mumbled. "Not without my…" Her eyelids drooped. *Permission.*

Water dripped on Sally's forehead. She shivered, wiped it away, and rolled over, tugging the cloak-blanket with her. Rain pattered softly around her.

Drips echoed in her ear.

Plop.

The sounds muted. Water dribbled out of her ear and trickled down her neck.

Shafts of bright light danced around her. The gnome's silhouette blocked the opening of a shelter of large leaves erected around her.

Sally shoved the leaves aside. "You son of a—!"

"Good morning to you, as well." The gnome ran a whetstone along the blade of his axe and thumbed the edge.

"How dare you."

"You have your duties. I have mine." He handed her a jar. "It is my duty to take care of you." The sun glinted on the surface of the clear water. "Drink."

Sally glared at him. "How can I trust you?"

"You have not hydrated since yesterday morning. You are a nurse; you know humans need water to survive."

"Fine." She snatched the jar from him. Her teeth knocked the glass as she sipped. "Don't you ever sleep?"

He didn't answer.

"Or is that another Traveller superpower?"

He snorted.

"I have sent the bees to find the safest path to the source of the smoke." He scanned the sky as if he'd heard something, and lowered his voice. "They should return soon." He hefted his axe. "I hope."

Sally's stomach grumbled louder and more often. It'd been four days with no decent meal, and no more of the gnome's buns or toffees left to dull the hunger.

Patches of sunlight grew bigger, and brighter, as the forest thinned. They made faster time through the forest now.

Sally paused, occasionally, and leaned on her staff to rest her feet and allow the sun to warm her skin. Wind whistled between the tree trunks.

She fancied she heard the occasional tinkle of bells; she also fancied she saw the gnome duck under the cover of trees when she did so. She forfeited the sun's warmth and kept to the cover of the trees, just in case.

The wind changed direction, and tugged at her hair. The sound of bells wafted on the wind. And the faint sound of...

Singing?

A Christmas carol - the same one she'd heard bleeding from the portal in the glade.

Sally's heart skipped; perhaps there was another portal leading home?

She stepped off the path.

Once she'd found Alfred, it'd be a faster route home. They'd not last another four days trekking back to the Portal Glade without provisions.

Large drips of water dribbled off leaves onto the ground, soaking into her bandages. She pushed them aside with her staff, and picked her way through the undergrowth, following the music - away from the bees and the gnome.

After a few minutes, an overgrown track became visible. She followed it through the undergrowth. The light faded. The trees grew closer, circling a small rise. The spongy ground squelched and sank under her weight.

The song grew louder.

A curt buzz niggled at her periphery. A lone bee whizzed about her head. She swatted it away.

It darted back, then dashed directly at her. Its wings hummed and its body twitched as it hovered in front of her, pushing forward to slow her down. Its agitated buzz became more insistent.

But the music beckoned.

The portal was so close.

The bee flitted around her ear, the music drowning out its protests.

"Leave me alone," she growled. "I have to find the portal." She flicked it away. "It could be Alfred's only hope."

The bee sped away.

She walked towards the copse of trees near the top of the mound.

A glint of white flashed in the darkness, keeping its distance. She caught a few strains of its growling caw amongst the music, but continued on.

Leaf litter piled up against the tree trunks. Wood squeaked as they nudged each other. Branches swayed in the wind above. Fleeting specks of light danced over the ground, providing glimpses of pale, half-spherical objects half-

hidden in the leaves and clinging to their trunks.

Leaves fell on the mound and swirled up in eddies, funnelling around the trees.

Bioluminescent fungi, twice the size of her hands, extended on long stalks from smaller mounds of ground cover. Their gills glowed a pale, fluorescent lime green, their intensity ebbing and flowing with the music.

The colours shifted, taking on a bluish hue, similar to that of the swirling light of the portal.

She took another step and leaned closer.

The fungi trembled. Their caps swelled, doubling in size. Their colours swirled, mimicking the Glade Portal's movements as they coalesced into a doorway.

A way home.

Sally dropped her walking staff and reached out towards the portal.

A gloved hand wrenched her back from the growing gateway and grappled her to the ground. A second hand clamped over her mouth and nose.

The smell of leather pressed into her nostrils.

Metal rattled as they rolled down the mound. Her hair entangled her neck and whipped into her eyes, obscuring her vision.

They landed with a jolt, in a thicket of thorns. Pain shot along Sally's arm. She screamed. A heavy weight fell on her and knocked the breath from her lungs.

Silence.

Bang!

The sound of escaping gas filled the air.

Sally squirmed under the weight. And found an opening. She twisted onto her injured arm, and growled. Her knee smashed into the assailant's groin.

A deep groan. A clatter of metal, and the weight rolled off her chest, but the hand held fast over her face.

She gasped for air.

She clawed at the hand and pulled, trying to pry it away.

A grunt, but the hand remained. It was too strong.

She kicked again.

A weight pinned down her leg. She still had one last attack.

Sally sank her teeth into naked wrist, above the glove.

It jerked away.

Sally screamed as soon as she was free. "Get off me!"

Now the bastard was unbalanced, she lashed out. Hard. Launching him back towards the mound.

Metal scraped. Her attacker rolled onto his feet and blocked her way to the portal.

"Death's head on a—"

It was the gnome. Blocking her path to the portal.

"Out of my way." She sprang to her feet and surged towards the shrinking gateway. "I need to get home."

The gnome started towards her, glanced at his hand in horror, and froze. He stripped off his glove and flicked it into the portal.

"What about Alfred?" he snapped.

"Who?" Sally searched for a way past him.

"The reason why I followed you into this world," he replied.

"Let me pass."

He shook his head. "I cannot."

There! A gap between the shrubs. She feinted to his left.

He side-stepped to block her.

She dodged the other way and lunged towards the gap.

His movement was a blur.

She halted mid-step, and shook with rage.

"I order you to let me—"

He spun and kicked out, catching Sally on her side. She overbalanced and fell to the ground. The shock ricocheted down her arm.

The portal collapsed.

Gone.

A smell of ozone lingered.

Sally crumpled to the ground. Her hair fell over her face.

The stench of decay overwhelmed her. She pressed the back of her hand against her nostrils to dull the smell.

"Where?" She shook her head. "What?"

The fungi's light faded to dim points of green light.

The gnome stepped closer.

"You were enchanted," he replied in a gentle voice. "*Forest Fairies*, some call them. We call them *Ghost Makers*. They warp your mind and lure you in close enough to…"

He indicated a cloud of luminous, pale green, powder-like specks slowly drifting down and settling onto the ground where she'd stood. Shrivelled fungi wilted on decaying mounds under the dead husks of trees. Amongst them, was the gnome's discarded glove, the back of the hand and fingers dusted with the pale green powder, now covered with embryonic fungi, their stems skewering the leather and rooting it to the ground.

Sally scrambled back and covered her mouth.

Nearby were the remains of a small creature, not unlike the one she'd seen poisoned at the edge of the glade. A healthy crop of mushrooms - *Ghost Makers* - sprang from its decomposing corpse.

"They show you what you most desire," he said.

Sally's stomach churned, and heaved. She leaned forward, letting her hair fall over her face to hide her tears.

"But it was so real," she whispered. "There was no portal?"

"No portal."

"Why didn't it affect you?" She scoffed. "I suppose that's another of your superpowers?"

He turned to face her. Beads of perspiration clung to his forehead. His jaw clenched.

She stared into his dark eyes. There was pain there.

"No." His lip twitched. "But I am familiar with Otherworld enchantments."

She wiped a tear from her cheek and rocked back onto her heels.

"If you knew, why did you endanger yourself?"

"It is my duty," he replied.

"You have a choice, you know?"

"You are a Protector. I will give my life to save you, as the Protectors did to save my people."

He offered her his gloved hand.

She bowed her head in acknowledgment. Her mind raced. He'd risked his life to save her.

The childhood memory, the nightmares that haunted her for over two decades, came flooding back; but this time the blur of garden gnomes was not attacking her, but protecting her. Surrounding her. Covering her. Guarding her from the terror in the night.

She swallowed. She was only ten years old, blinded with panic and creating her own narrative to protect her mind from something she wasn't ready to understand.

"Thank you." She took his hand and rose to her feet. "*Red.*"

Red arched an eyebrow, handed her the walking staff. He bowed his head in reply.

"We best leave." He grasped his axe in both hands. He tilted his head in the direction of the fungi. "They will not be pleased to be denied a nursery for their young'uns."

"You speak as if they're sentient."

"They are." He pointed his axe in the opposite direction. "After you, Protector."

"Please, call me Sally," she said.

"After you, Sally."

They followed the lone bee along the overgrown path.

"How did you find me?"

"The bee warned me of the danger." A smile flickered across his lips. "She's taken a liking to you."

"Oh." There was a vague memory of a very persistent bug. She sucked in a sharp breath. "Remind me to apologise to her."

The gnome's smile grew into a grin.

"I am sure she will understand."

chapter ten

The patches of light grew more frequent as they trekked through the forest. A worn path slowly emerged: a slight holloway worn into the ground wound between the trees.

The continuous din of cicadas faded, replaced by tweets and chirrups of avian inhabitants in the canopy above.

Giant dragonflies flitted in and out of the light, their wings glinting in the sun.

Sally's mood lifted with the increased light, and the enthusiastic companionship of her personal bee guide.

The bees seemed cheerier, too. They buzzed amongst themselves. Two peeled away from the babble and sped ahead.

Another drifted back to join Sally and Red. It buzzed around her Guardian's ear.

He nodded. "They have gone to scout ahead to make sure there are no…" He gripped his axe tightly, "surprises."

Specks of blazing sunlight winked further along the path. They slowed their pace.

She could see the edge of the forest now. Sunlight dazzled through the leaves and danced across the path. Daylight beckoned.

Flowers crept into the forest along the path, drinking in the sunlight and spilled out to a vast plain of undulating yellow grass. A faint whiff of wood smoke carried on the wind.

Odd, bird-like creatures circled at the edge of the trees. Their feathers shimmered in the sun.

The bees darted back into the shadows, away from the edge of the forest.

Sally's personal bee twitched. *Danger*.

Red halted. He glanced skyward, and swung his satchel away from his axe-arm.

She could hear it now.

Sleigh bells.

Another turn in the path. Sunlight bathed the ground ahead.

The smell of wood smoke was strong now.

Sally's heart dropped. Heat flashed over her skin. She clenched her walking staff. She wanted to run. To hide in the shadows.

"It cannot see us." He clasped her hands in his. "But, for precaution's sake," he squeezed her fingers, "best we stay under cover."

The jingle of sleigh bells and the slow whoosh of wings grew louder.

Sally crouched behind a tree and waited.

The shadow rippled along the grass. Circling. Bells tinkled, faded, and returned - over and over; each rush of wind jostled the leaves around them.

It was close.

Leaves crunched to her left.

Sally froze.

Another crunch. Too light to match the size of the shadow creature.

"It is gone." Red's deep voice was reassuring.

The bees flanked him, buzzing quietly. Her personal bee guide hummed supportively by her shoulder.

She rose slowly. and peered beyond the trees. The birds glided back to frolic in the sunlight.

"Are you sure?" she asked.

He strode to the edge of the tree line and searched the sky with his spyglass. "I am sure."

Sally crept out from her cover and joined him.

The countryside of swaying yellow grass stretched for kilometres, dipping into valleys between low, rolling hills.

Small mobs of *Not-Cows*, unaffected by the grass, grazed under scattered stands of wide, flat trees. They prodded straying younglings back under the tree cover with the long horn in the centre of their foreheads. Long-billed bird-like creatures milled around them, hopping from back to back, and burying their curved needle-like bills into the *Not-cows'* thick hair.

A pine wood lined the horizon.

"There aren't many places to hide, if the creature returns," said Sally.

"I can see that." Red grunted.

Wind whipped over the grass, blustered around Sally's legs, and lifted her skirt. She shivered. With no protection from the trees, it chilled her to the bone.

She pulled the gnome's cloak close, aware her bare calves

and shoe-less feet were more exposed to the grass' toxic sap.

Red was at her side.

"Is everything all right?" asked Red. "Are you *sure* you want to do this?"

"It's just the chill," she replied.

The wind changed direction, pulling the long grass with it, revealing a faint dirt road, a few metres wide, winding over the crest of a low hill and off to the south - at least it felt like it was south.

Tendrils of grey woodsmoke twisted into the sky above the pine wood.

"Over there." Sally pointed in the direction of the smoke. "Do you see it?"

"I saw it," replied Red.

"Perhaps we can find help there?"

Red shook his head.

"I know." She sighed. "We can't assume they're friendly."

The bees circled around them, as if to push them on. Sally took a tentative step forward.

Red didn't move. "Are you sure?"

Her teeth chattered. Smoke meant fire, and fire meant warmth. She eyed the gathering clouds. She imagined a crackling fire and dry clothes and hoped Alfred had already found them.

"We have to find Alfred," she replied. "Or do you have a better idea?"

The bees buzzed in agreement.

Red scowled at them. "It is not safe. We do not know who, or what, we will find there." He frowned. "But we cannot stand here and wait for the creature to return." He unhooked his axe. "But you are the Protector. It is your decision."

Sally's stomach knotted. What would Aunt Enid do?

Her friendly bee landed and pirouetted on her shoulder.

In the distance, a faint white speck circled above the road. It hovered for a moment, then continued along the road towards the wood on the horizon.

Red didn't react; he hadn't seen it. She massaged the bridge of her nose. *Obviously, a hallucination.* Red had said they lingered.

"Aunt Enid said I should trust the bees, that they'll show me the way." She swallowed. "We follow the smoke."

Red sighed. "That is your decision, then?"

She nodded. "Alfred would've done the same."

The hills hadn't looked high, but traipsing up and down them had taken a toll on Sally's leg muscles.

They'd walked for hours, avoiding the grass and listening for sleigh bells to warn them of the creature's return. Fortunately, it seemed to have grown bored with them.

The tree line seemed just as far as it had when they'd started out. Sally had a feeling of *déjà vu*, like crossing the Hay Plains - but without the benefit of a car.

The clouds hovered on - what she assumed was - the north horizon. They darkened and coalesced into a thick bank. Flashes of light crackled inside them as they crept closer.

Sally rested her walking staff against a tree. Its low, wide canopy shielded her from the wind in a hollow between the hills.

She leaned against the trunk and lifted one foot off the ground. Dust and small stones had worked their way between the bandages and dug into her skin. She picked them out from between the wrappings, and massaged the soles.

"Problem?" Red halted ahead of her. "We should try to make the cover of the trees before the storm hits."

Sally's bee friend lifted off her shoulder, kissing her cheek gently with its wings, and hummed reassuringly.

She took a deep breath, letting its borrowed-calmness fill her lungs, and relax her muscles.

"Thank you, Beatriz." She grabbed her staff, gritted her teeth as she redistributed her weight onto both feet, and strode past Red. "Come on."

The road turned north, towards the clouds.

The humid air pressed in around them. The temperature had dropped. Bea snuggled closer on Sally's shoulder.

In the distance, the clouds grumbled. So did Sally's stomach. They'd been walking since breakfast - or it would've been breakfast if they'd had any food.

Red led them over another hill. A narrow stream flowed along the valley. The road widened, turned again, away from the clouds, and followed the stream through the valley and into the wood.

Sally stretched her feet. Only a little further; just over one more small hill and she could rest her feet and warm the chill from her bones.

Bea raced down the hill to tell Red to slow down.

Wood smoke curled skyward, from just inside the edge of the trees. A glint of white caught in the sunlight. It flew along the stream and entered the wood.

The raven was back, leading them into the wood, towards the source of the smoke, to find Alfred. It couldn't be a hallucination?

Sally hobbled down the hill to join Red and the bees. She

couldn't see the forest from the valley; neither Red, nor the bees, would have seen the raven.

They followed the road along the creek towards the pine wood. Brilliant aqua and pink flowers, with long strappy maroon leaves, grew along the water's edge. Small silver, aquatic creatures slipped along with the current, jumping amongst the trickling water.

Sally's stomach groaned. She eyed them and sighed. "I don't suppose we could eat fish for dinner?"

Red shook his head. "Best not eat—"

"I know." Sally's shoulders slumped. "But a girl can hope."

The wood was thick with pine trees. The road narrowed as they ventured deeper. Needles crunched under their feet. The birds sounded different here; quieter, more wary. And the cicadas… there were none.

A bell jingled up ahead.

"Do not move!"

Sally froze mid-step. Her heart plunged into her stomach. The shadow creature was here!

Beatriz flitted behind her. The rest of the bees took cover on a branch above them.

Red crouched low, crept up beside her, flattened his back against a trunk, and scanned the trees.

Sally was exposed. Alone.

The ringing faded.

Bea slowly drifted along the track.

Red pressed a finger to his lips and plucked at a fine silk thread caught taut by Sally's ankle. The bell jingled ahead of them again.

Bea darted back and landed on Sally's shoulder.

"It is a warning system." He traced his finger along the thread around the base of a trunk.

Sally lowered her foot slowly.

"Or," Red glanced over his shoulder, the thread still hooked over one finger, "it could be a booby trap."

The thread wound its way away from the track through several eyes and pulleys.

"Wait here," he said. "And do not move."

A few minutes later, he returned. He hooked his un-gloved thumb under his belt. "Well, it is a trap."

The bees swarmed around her.

Red chuckled and snapped the thread.

Sally sucked in a sharp breath.

The bells jingled furiously.

"What the—?"

"The bells attract any hungry creatures roaming around." He gestured back into the woods, in the direction he'd investigated. "They lure them towards a series of hanging baskets of food, over there."

At the mention of food, Sally's stomach complained.

"The smoke is stronger this way," he said.

Red continued along the path, slower this time, sweeping the path and lifting clumps of pine needle litter and nudging stones with the tip of his axe.

Sally stepped over the broken thread, and followed him.

A few hundred metres down the track, they passed by two water-stained wicker baskets hanging by ropes from a tree branch. They'd seen better days.

"We must be getting close," replied Red. "Tread

carefully."

Soon, wisps of grey smoke curled around the trees, shrouding the path. The bees rose higher, above the smoke. It became denser as they walked, spreading out into the trees as far as they eye could see.

"A bushfire?" She hesitated. Bushfires were all too common back home in the Adelaide Hills. From childhood, it'd been drilled into her: *don't go through smoke if you can't see the other side*.

Red sniffed the air. "I doubt it. I think we found your *civilisation*," he replied.

chapter eleven

ore food baskets hung from the trees along the track, partially hidden in the smoke, their location identified by the ripe aroma of rotting fruit.

Pinpoints of light gleamed in the haze ahead, glowing brighter as they walked on. Sally fanned away the last vestiges of smoke to reveal a small clearing bathed in sunlight.

Silver pine trees sparkled in the sun. Large globules of water collected at the ends of their branches and sparkled, like baubles.

Smoke leaked from the stone chimney of a quirky, oval cottage. Storm clouds crept over the clearing. Streams of sunlight broke and glinted off the surrounding trees, as if Aunt Agnes had been let loose in the Christmas Department and dragged home a haul of shiny ornaments and dumped them on a wall of foil Christmas trees.

The cottage squatted awkwardly at the centre of the clearing. It reminded Sally of a bloated toadstool: a thick layer of maroon moss grew over its rounded roof. Dark grey stone tiles peeked through bald patches, and clumps of white flowers dotted the moss.

Two oval windows were visible on either side of a wooden door. Pink stains marred the white-plastered walls where water had washed through the moss and dribbled down.

A small, glowing ball of orange light hovered several metres above the chimney, collecting the smoke and funnelling it downwards into the surrounding trees, feeding the low-lying smoke concealing the area around the clearing.

A smaller maroon-mossed turret peeked out from the opposite side of the cottage.

"Stay here." Red crept back into the smoke. A twig cracked not far away.

Then silence.

A creature croaked in the smoke.

Wind whispered through the trees. Leaves danced and rustled. Wood creaked around her as the treetops swayed, dislodging the water baubles from the pine branches and splashing them onto the ground.

A branch splintered on the other side of the cottage.

The wind stopped.

The glowing ball above the chimney flickered. The smoke stopped moving.

Again, silence.

The light ball crackled with a renewed burst of light, its colour taking on a pink hue.

A flight of dark, leather-winged creatures launched into the air, squawking and dodging the light ball, and escaped over the trees.

There was an annoyed grunt beside her.

"A few more of the baskets." Red's voice was a deep whisper. "But no more traps." He untangled a silk thread from the head of his axe. "And a small vegetable garden behind the cottage."

A prolonged gurgle rumbled deep in Sally's stomach. "Perhaps we could just—"

He sucked in a sharp breath through his teeth.

Sally hugged her stomach and closed her eyes, trying not to think of her aunt's gingerbread, scones and lemon butter - oh, and Alfred's divine-smelling fruitcake he'd brought over for Christmas dinner.

"Surely, something from the garden would be safe?" she asked.

"Your aunt said—"

"I know, I know."

Sally remained by his side as he moved forward. A faint hum reverberated in her ears. Another step, and a buzz washed over her, making the hair stand on the back of her arms.

The world wobbled and went silent for a moment. Then her foot was on the ground again, and the sounds of the wood engulfed her.

She shook her head. Red scanned the clearing as he moved forward.

The bees lagged behind, hovering at the edge of the woods. Bea circled in front of them.

"Looks like your theory about Mr Knowles searching out the smoke was correct." He pointed at the soft ground. "Tracks." He continued on, following the tracks closely. "He is about six foot two, yes?"

Sally checked the calculations in her head. Approximately one hundred and eighty-eight centimetres. "Yes."

"Then, he was running."

They were halfway across the clearing now. Sally examined the tracks nearby.

"How can you tell?" she asked.

"Long stride." He knelt beside the closest one. "And the toe is deeper."

She scanned the tracks. There was a second set, like those they'd seen earlier.

"Is that another Howler?" she asked.

"Yes," he replied. "They were both running."

"Was it chasing him?"

"I doubt it," he replied. "They were both running and dodging something and, see there?" The tracks parallelled each other, heading towards the cottage.

"So, what was chasing them?" she asked.

Red shrugged. "There are no other tracks."

"The shadow creature?" she whispered.

He glanced at the sky and hefted his axe.

"Walk where I walk."

Howler tracks circled the house. A few fragments of torn, frayed material - and another of red silk - clung to the step.

Sally stifled a gasp with her hand. They were too close to the cottage; any noise could alert those inside.

"It attacked Alfred?" she whispered.

"They are Travellers, like me. They are usually helpful, but… they can be unpredictable and they have a mischievous sense of humour." He gripped his axe and glanced into the trees. "But do not usually attack humans." He re-directed his attention to the front of the cottage, then pointed out the faint traces of dry, muddy footprints on the cottage steps. "He made it to safety."

Sally smiled with relief. "You're sure?"

"These are days old." He frowned and rose slowly. "And there are no human tracks leading away. Only Howler tracks, running back into the woods."

Red edged towards the door and pressed his ear against it.

The hinges creaked.

Sally cringed.

He raised an eyebrow and pushed the door. It shuddered and swung open a crack.

The enticing aroma of ginger, honey, and fresh lemon wafted out on a stream of warm air. Her stomach rumbled.

She inhaled deeply. It smelled of home. Her entire body relaxed.

She peered over Red's shoulder, her eyes taking a few seconds to adjust to the dim light.

It was a snug room, with white daubed walls framed with a skeleton of dark wood. Arched windows of sooty glass, wiped clean in a few areas, allowed a view of the path.

Under the window to the right, half-hidden behind the open door, was a wooden bench stacked with ceramic plates and earthenware mugs. A bowl of vibrant-coloured, mostly odd-looking fruit - and a few yellow, ovoid fruits resembling lemons - sat in the middle. Floral curtains hid the contents under the bench.

A low fire crackled in a stone fireplace surround on the centre wall of the cottage. A mound of fired clay pots was piled on the floor stones in front of the hearth.

"I can't hear anyone," said Red.

Sally reached over him and pushed the door open all the way.

Sunlight streamed across the earth floor. Dried flowers

and grasses hung from the roof's central wooden beam. Small clay pots of fresh herbs lined the window, wiped clean allowing more light onto the workbench. The only metal item in the entire room was a large pot from the side of the fireplace.

An open doorway was in the middle of the opposite wall, next to a round kitchen table. Two chairs sat on the other side of the table; one tucked neatly under the table, the other had fallen back and balanced on its back legs against the wall.

Red nudged aside a pair of blue leather boots near the doorway, and stepped into the room.

A single candle flickered on the table. Its shadow danced over a tray of gingerbread, in the shape of fairies, smelling like it'd just come out of the oven. Beside them was a plate heaped with generous slices of fruitcake; one half-eaten. Gingerbread crumbs dusted the table where the chair had overbalanced.

Sally licked her lips.

"Your friend must have been as hungry as you are," said Red.

The window clicked. A cool breeze drifted across the bench and the table, catching the smell of baked goodness and circled back, bringing with it the mouthwatering aroma. It tickled her nostrils, inviting her to eat. Her stomach grumbled. It was willing.

She could taste the ginger, feel the smooth texture rolling in her mouth, bursting with brown sugar and golden syrup; just like Aunt Enid made.

She reached out her hand…

"Stop!"

Sally froze.

"Do not eat anything," growled Red. He indicated the table in front of the overturned chair.

A china teacup. How had she not noticed it?

"Look familiar?" he asked.

Sally nodded. It was much like her aunt's favourite set, but with distorted pink flowers in place of roses. She snatched back her hand.

"*Magick*," he whispered. "It is always harder to delve into the mind of creatures from other worlds than your own. You can never get the details quite right."

He raised his axe, and inched past the fireplace, careful to keep out of view of the door on the other side, and glanced into the room beyond. He lowered his axe and rejoined her.

"He is not in there."

Red ran his fingers over the crumbs, pressed one onto his fingertip, and sniffed. He closed his eyes and smiled.

Sally's hand gravitated towards the tray. The heavenly aroma of her aunt's gingerbread beckoned her. Her hand trembled.

His firm grip stayed her hand.

"What do you smell?" he asked.

"Aunt Enid's gingerbread."

"I smell… dandelion and oat cakes. My pairb—" He drew in a long breath. "My favourite."

He guided her hand back to her side.

"We are agreed *magick* is at work here," he said, finally.

She nodded in agreement. Her stomach gurgled its dissent.

Her mouth watered.

Concentrate. There was something important she'd

forgotten; something she had to find.

She frowned. Red was right; there was *magick* at work.

She gripped the back of the overturned chair; if her hands were occupied, she couldn't take one of the…

She shook her head, flipped up the chair, and slid it under the table.

Something scraped along the floor. She checked under the table. A Shoe. Italian leather. No metal; the eyelets punched directly into the leather. Undamaged by the portal, but severely scuffed and caked in mud.

Alfred!

Memories are a funny thing. She'd seen it many times in the ED, particularly with patients who'd suffered extreme shock or trauma: the sudden rush of realisation when a memory snapped back. Everyone reacted differently; some were embarrassed, some in denial, and some with an obsessive focus.

"I *have* to find Alfred," she blurted out as she charged into the other room.

The cottage's stone-worked turret partially blocked the window, casting a shadow across the room and allowing in little natural light. A fireplace crackled cheerfully behind its grate on the stone tiled floor.

Under an uncurtained window, sat an over-stuffed lounge chair with dozens of soft, comfy cushions. Tucked in the right-hand corner was a small, triangular desk brimming with lop-sided stacks of books shoved against the walls.

Suspended above the desk, and crammed into a small shelf above, were various skeletons of small creatures, some vaguely familiar and some curiously alien.

Glass jars full of squashed, unrecognisable contents suspended in green liquid - some a little too skin-like in colour for her comfort - lined its edges along the walls on either side.

Ceramic mugs and jars, and a set of glass test tubes were wedged in a wooden stand with various coloured, dried contents splashed up their insides.

Scribbled notes were fanned across the table next to a glass ink container with the writing quill still standing inside ready for use, filled with unrecognisable symbols, the last lines still shining in the firelight.

Sally touched the last symbol on the page and examined her fingertip. A faint smudge of black ink remained on it, still slightly wet; someone had been here not long ago. Yet the cottage seemed abandoned.

She turned slowly, looking for possible hiding places. Stone floor tiles had been removed beneath a large, full-length mirror hanging on the wall, revealing the bare soil. Paint peeled from the edges of long claw marks scoring the mirror's ancient, ornate frame. A large crack ran down its centre, revealing what appeared to be a silvered backing.

A second metal object. Sally frowned. How had it passed through the portal? She stepped forward and raised her hand to touch the surface. Shards of glass crunched on the bare soil.

She hesitated. *Best not*; Red's voice echoed in her head.

She back away and spied Alfred's shredded waistcoat shoved into a rubbish basket beside the mirror. She snatched it up and spun frantically, searching for any signs of what had happened to him.

A curtain fluttered to her left. A step led up to a doorway. She pulled the curtain to the side. There was another room.

A door slammed behind her. She wheeled towards the sound.

"Sally." It was Red's voice in the kitchen. "I have found something."

"So have I."

Across the room another curtain slid open to reveal a second doorway. Wooden floorboards creaked under Red's heavy boots as he entered.

"It was hidden behind the open front door."

A bed dominated the room. Near its foot was a curtained window. And on the bed was—

"Alfred!"

He was cold. And pale. Deathly pale.

"No, no, no." She grabbed his wrist and searched for a pulse. She shifted her fingers and applied more pressure. Her heart pounded.

Wait. There it was. Faint, but there. And racing very fast.

A tear rimmed her eyelid. She'd found him; but was it too late? It looked like he'd lost a lot of blood.

She squeezed her eyelids closed, trying to erase the vision of Alfred, dead.

Her hands trembled. She berated herself; she'd handled worse at work. Why was this any different?

"Because he is a close friend," Red's voice whispered in her ear. "And you feel responsible for him."

"How did you—?"

He raised an eyebrow.

She clenched her jaw, and pushed up Alfred's sleeves and trouser legs, looking for any signs of injury. Faint gravel rash scars were still visible on his forearms from his heroic actions against The Dark, last summer, and on his chest, were three faint silvery lines where Mr B had come to her defence.

A speck of blood marred his shirt collar. She peeled it away, preparing herself for a lot of blood. Alfred's blood.

She brushed her fingers over his skin. She smiled slowly. Other than a couple of spots on the inside of the collar, there was no blood; what there was, were two needle marks. She pressed their edges with her fingertips. They were slightly wider than expected for needle punctures.

Red leaned closer. "That is not good."

"You know what did this?"

He shook his head. "But draining blood is never good."

She ran through the list of possible creatures she knew of, which could create a bi-punctured wound. First on the list was—

"Do vampires exist?" she squeaked.

"It could be any of several Otherworldly creatures," he answered.

"You didn't answer my question." *Again.*

He rose slowly and sniffed the air. "Does not smell like *The Cursed*. Besides, there are too many windows. Too much sunlight."

"Then what?" she asked.

"There are many creatures who require such sustenance."

He slipped the shoe onto Alfred's foot and circled the room to a third door on the outer wall, listened, then opened it slowly, axe at the ready.

It smelled of rose water and lavender.

"Bathroom." He returned to the foot of the bed, nudged

a wooden chest out of the way to reach the curtain, and cinched up a corner of the curtain to look out. "We need to set wards. Do you remember your aunt's protection spell?"

Sally glared at him. "No magic, remember?"

She swallowed. There was one other option; she'd have to admit she'd searched his satchel without permission.

"How about a protection circle?" she asked. "We could use the salt in your satchel."

"You went through my things?" He glared at her.

"Sorry, I… I was looking… I needed…" Her cheeks burned.

"We will talk about this later," he growled. "I doubt it would work anyway." He stared back out the window.

Sally returned her attention to Alfred. Her mind reeled, listing procedures for hypervolemic shock:

One: prevent loss of body heat
Two: wound above the heart
Three: elevate feet
Four: IV fluids
Five: iron rich foods
Six: immobilise and
Seven: sleep as much as possible.

The last was problematic; his captor could return at any moment.

She felt Alfred's cheeks with the back of her hand.

"He's freezing." She spread her cloak over him. "Alfred, wake up. It's Sally." And to Red, she said: "We need to get him to a hospital."

She chose to ignore the fact they were four days walk from the portal, with no food. Well, none they could eat.

But, first, he needed fluids. Surely, there was a well?

A sudden thought chilled her blood; was he in a coma? That'd mean he'd lost - she calculated the numbers in her head… way too much blood.

She sat on the bed and checked his pupils.

"I need a light." They'd lost the light sticks in the swamp, and the remaining flash stick would not last long enough. She glanced up at the window; Red's face was bathed in the sunlight.

"The mirror," she said. "In the study. It's broken. Fetch me a shard."

The curtain fell back in place, darkening the room again. Red strode into the study and returned with a small shard.

"Hold up the curtain." She opened lifted Alfred's eyelids and noted the small pupils. "Reflect the sunlight into each one, for a second."

He followed her instructions.

Bilateral, reactive pupils. Sally rocked back on the bed. Most likely no brain damage.

Red was at the head of the bed now. Another small cake plate and a fired-clay mug were on the bedside table. He lifted the mug and sniffed.

"He has been drugged. A concoction of valerian, chamomile, lavender and," he frowned, "a hallucinogen."

"The sap?" She shook Alfred's shoulders. "But you said—"

Red placed the mirror shard in front of Alfred's mouth. Fog flashed over the glass, ebbing and renewing with each breath. He sniffed the mug again.

"There is only a hint. Smells more like the same substance as the fungi. Just enough to lower his mental defences, and control his dreams."

A shiver ran along Sally's spine. She remembered how real the hallucination had been.

"Wake up, Alfred." She shook his shoulders again. "It's not real."

His eyes fluttered under his eyelids.

"We need to get fluids into him."

"Already on it." Red fetched a cup from the kitchen, filled it with water from one of his jars, and pulled a small vial from his satchel. It glowed green. He poured the fluorescent liquid into the cup and swirled it.

Sally blocked his hand. "Are you sure?"

"Trust me."

"Please, wake up," she said. "You need to drink this."

Red hovered at her shoulder, antidote ready in hand.

"Perhaps try your *magick*?" he whispered.

She shook her head. "Doesn't work, remember?"

Lightning flashed across the curtain. Thunder rumbled. A shadow flickered outside.

"The creature?" Sally flexed her fingers. "Not now," she growled under her breath.

She leaned next to Alfred's ear and spoke as loud as she dared. "Wake up, Alfred!"

His eyes stilled under their lids.

"I know you can hear me," she hissed through clenched teeth. "Wake up, damn it. Aunt Enid will kill me if I don't get you back home."

Red slapped Alfred's face.

Alfred's eyelids twitched and flicked open.

"There you go," said Red.

Sally slipped her free arm under his neck and raised his head. "Here, drink this."

Red pressed the jar to Alfred's lips and poured the antidote slowly.

Alfred gulped down the liquid and spluttered. "What the—?" he grumbled.

"Please, it will help you feel better," said Sally.

Red tilted the jar further.

Alfred sipped slowly.

"Enid…" Alfred pushed Red's hand away. "Who are…?"

He jerked upright on the bed. The wooden slats squeaked under his weight. He shook his head and blinked.

"Sally?" He grabbed his head and groaned. "God, that tasted disgusting." He grimaced.

"It means it's good for you," she replied.

He scoffed. "You sound like your great aunt."

"I'll take that as a compliment," she replied.

"You need to rest while we work out a plan." She glanced at Red. "You do have a plan?"

He considered a moment. "Yes. But you are not going to like it."

Sally sat on the edge of the bed next to Alfred. He moaned, his head buried in his hands.

Red had removed the last of her foot bandages. Thin, silvery lines marked where the now-healed lacerations had been.

"That salve is miraculous. What did you put in it?" she said.

"That sling needs fixing." He wrapped up the used bandages.

Sally huffed. Again, he'd avoided answering her.

She slipped her arm out of its sling and flexed her fingers. Pain ripped along the tendons. She gritted her teeth, trying not to show the pain, and handed it to him.

He glanced at her forearm as he re-knotted the sling. "How is the arm?"

"It could use some salve," she replied.

He clicked his tongue. "Only good for minor abrasions, I am afraid." He slipped the sling over her head. "Your arm needs *magick*."

"You know I can't channel magic without an amulet," she tucked her arm back into the sling, "or a Focus."

"We need to get Mr Knowles out of here," said Red.

"I'm not going anywhere dressed like this," said Sally. She'd need something more than a torn, cotton sundress to protect her from the soporific grass sap when they returned to the glade.

She rose and walked to the end of the bed, avoiding his accusatory gaze, and ferreted through the chest for suitable clothing.

"I need to change." She opened the bathroom door. "I won't be long."

Sally pulled at the embroidered cuffs of the heavy linen shirt and hitched up the tan trousers. Their owner was definitely taller, and stouter, than she was.

She closed the bathroom door, slipped on the borrowed green jacket, and stepped over a newly-made salt circle hugging the edges of the room.

"We cannot stay here forever," said Red. "He needs medical attention."

"I know," she whispered.

Alfred wobbled and listed to one side. Sally caught his shoulder before he could fall back onto the bed.

"Alfred?" She checked his pulse. Barely there. Red's antidote wouldn't reverse Alfred's blood loss.

Another shadow flickered across the curtain.

Sally's heart beat against her ribcage.

Her fingers buzzed.

Red moved to the foot of the bed, lifted the curtain a crack, and peered through the window. His gaze tracked something across the sky.

"Is it…?"

He chewed his bottom lip, retrieved his axe and nodded.

"Shit." She eased Alfred's legs over the edge of the bed. "Do you think you can walk?" she asked him.

Alfred tried to lift his foot. The strain was obvious. He shook his head.

Red turned his back to the window.

Wings flapped outside.

Heat pricked Sally's skin. Sparks crackled at her fingertips. She scowled, flicked away the pain and ducked her left shoulder under Alfred's arm.

"Could you?" She strained under Alfred's weight. "I need help."

Red slipped his arm around Alfred's waist. Alfred fumbled for Red's shoulder.

"Here, use this." Red grabbed Sally's walking stick and tucked it under Alfred's other arm.

Red led the way through the curtained door to the kitchen and paused to check the window before opening the door.

"What is it?" she asked.

He touched a finger to his lips. "It is waiting for us," he whispered.

He nudged the door open a few centimetres.

Storm clouds had gathered above the cottage. Lightning crackled. Thunder vibrated the walls as the smell of ozone enveloped them.

The sound of flapping wings grew louder.

Sally peered out the kitchen window. There was no sign of the creature. "It must be directly above us."

The fire flared in the kitchen's hearth. She wiped her forehead with the back of her hand.

Red's gaze followed her hand.

"We will have to make a run for it," he said.

"On three?" she asked.

Alfred struggled to keep balance between Sally and the makeshift crutch.

"Don't think I'll make it," he mumbled. "Leave me behind."

Sally repositioned herself under his arm and hissed at Red. "Wait."

His hand remained on the door. "We would move faster if you tried your magic."

Sally stiffened. "I can't."

He searched the sky outside. "We have no chance like this. You *must* try."

She held her breath. The lightning was getting closer. The air buzzed around her. The hair on her arms pricked. She reached for the friendship bracelet to calm her panic. Her wrist was bare. It was gone.

Her heart raced. She closed her eyes. She'd have to do this another way. She scanned the room, looking for five things to list. She exhaled and shook her head.

"I can't. Not without my amulet," she said.

Rain pattered against the window pane.

Alfred wobbled, his face ashen.

Sally searched his eyes: Fatigue. Confusion. Fear.

"He won't make it," she whispered to Red.

"You don't look so great yourself." Alfred frowned.

"Hush." Red shifted his weight between his feet as if gauging the timing.

The hinges creaked as he opened the door slowly.

Large rain drops splashed on the stone step.

Another rumble of thunder vibrated through her chest.

Red smiled. "It is now or never."

Wings flapped above them - louder this time - as if to emphasise his words.

Sally grabbed for the fancy blue boots behind the door.

"No time to put them on now," he growled.

"I won't make it back through that grass without them."

He snatched them up, waited for a few seconds, then launched himself into the rain.

"Ready?" She whispered in Alfred's ear.

He swallowed and nodded.

They shuffled through the door.

Menacing storm clouds circled above them. Bright red clouds glowed pink and purple with each flash of lightning.

Her heart raced.

"Hurry," hissed Red. He grabbed Alfred's crutch and pulled, almost toppling him over. "We must hurry." He brandished his axe high and forged onward.

Sally hobbled out the door. Alfred struggled to keep up as they stumbled towards the safety of the wood. Red berated her with every step. She was useless without her amulet. And he knew it. Alfred would die. Aunt Enid would be devastated. And it would be her fault.

Rain drenched her face - camouflaging her tears. It soaked through her borrowed clothes, and dripped from her hair down her collar.

"We will not make it," he growled.

Heat flashed over her skin. If only she could shut up that blasted gnome. He had no idea how magic worked.

Another flap above them, almost drowning out the thunder. Sally flinched. Alfred ducked. His crutch slipped in the mud. He stumbled.

She wrenched him to his feet. They lurched forward. Red was on Alfred's other side, supporting him.

"This is all your fault," he growled. "A real Protector would know what to do."

"Don't." She clenched her teeth and cursed under her breath.

He smiled.

Arsehole. She *knew* he couldn't be trusted.

Sally's feet sizzled. The air crackled around her.

The flapping wings came closer, but she dared not look behind them.

They continued to run.

"This would be easier if you had your magic."

"Shut up!" *You damn garden gnome*. Burning pain coursed along her fingers.

She glanced towards the trees. *Too far away*.

The bees jiggled nervously near the edge of the wood, strangely silent.

Her heart sank. They'd never make it.

Just inside the wood, a flicker of white appeared behind the bees, coloured stones glinting at its throat. The raven had returned. The lightning reflected in its eyes. It flew back into the trees then returned, and hovered for a moment as if calling her to join it, then retreated into the shadow of the trees, again.

Exhaustion be damned. She was not going to fail Alfred. A burst of energy pulsed through her. She ran towards the trees, dragging Alfred with her.

The gnome trotted after them. "Your aunt would—"

Boom!

Thunderous force waves shuddered though Sally's body. She screamed.

Alfred was wrenched from under her and sent sprawling. Sally landed hard in the mud. The gnome pirouetted into the air and landed heavily on the ground behind her. Armour clanked.

She threw herself over Alfred to protect him. Her muscles tensed, expecting the shadow creature to descend upon them. But the onslaught never came.

The gnome's armour clattered as he pushed himself to his feet. His boots stomped past her. He swore.

"We are trapped."

Sally rose slowly. Alfred lay awkwardly at her feet. He moaned groggily.

A reverberating hum buzzed through her head. She'd heard that sound before, when they'd entered the clearing. The air had wobbled, like they'd walked through a… "Force field!"

Lightning cracked above them.

She swore and spun on her heel to face the gnome.

"You're the Traveller, the expert." Mud seeped between her toes. "How could you not know there was a *Ward* set?" She dug her toes deeper into the sludge. "You are supposed to be my Guardian. You were supposed to protect us."

The gnome's gaze darted over the clearing, then settled on her. "Your aunt would have known." His stare burrowed into her, accusingly. "This is your fault. You have no *magick*." He scoffed. "What made you think you were a Protector?"

"Don't!" Sally's blood boiled. Her fingers sizzled. Their muscles tensed as she formed a fist.

He glanced at her naked feet sinking into the mud, and smiled. He grabbed Alfred's arm, then hers, and ran towards the forcefield.

There was a bright flash. A deafening crack filled her ears as the smell of ozone enveloped her.

And the world convulsed.

chapter twelve

Everything disintegrated with a deafening, screeching hiss. Brilliant white light engulfed Sally, searing into her skin, and boiling her blood. Everything was white: the light, the noise, the wildfire running down her nerves; everything. And yet, there was nothing.

And she was alone.

Again.

She screamed. But there was no sound.

The light slowly dimmed and faded to a pale purple.

She lay on her back, the damp woollen coat now twisted around her feet. Every muscle rebelled.

Long sticky ribbons lashed at her trousers, at her sleeves. Her hair whipped around her face and caught in her throat. She clawed at her face and spat out the damp, clinging tendrils, thankful she'd 'borrowed' a change of clothes.

A howling wind replaced the hiss in her ears and, in the distance, the faint, high-pitched growling groan of a portal.

There was another groan, much closer.

Metal clanked behind her.

Sally dragged herself up onto her elbows. She was

surrounded by a sea of flailing yellow grass. The yellow grass. She was in the glade.

Her head swam. She gripped the ground, to steady herself and felt the wet coat beneath her hands. The smell of singed wool filled her nostrils.

"I knew you could do it!" The gnome's faced loomed above her, a mischievous grin plastered on his face.

"Do what?" She tugged at the coat around her feet.

"*Magick*, of course." Another grin. "*Wild Magick*." He dropped the blue leather boots beside her.

"But it's forbidden.' She extricated the twisted coat from her feet. "It's too…"

"Unpredictable?" he replied. "Yes, but there was no other option. We needed *magick*, and this place," he spread his arms wide, "is full of it." He offered her a hand up. "Though I thought you would have a connection with *T'erra*, like your aunt and Sylvia, not *F'nuen*.

Sally stared at her hands. Sparks still crackled between her fingers. Black specks of soot covered the tips. There were scorch marks on the coat where she'd touched it.

"Well, I…" The sparks fizzled into the air. She dropped her hands into her lap, and blinked. "Wait. Aunt Enid used *Wild Magick*?"

"Ah…" He avoided her gaze.

A moan came from within the grass nearby. They both spun towards it.

"That will be Mr Knowles," he said.

"Alfred!" How could she forget?

He lay sprawled in the grass a few metres away from them.

Sally pulled on the boots, and sucked in a shaky breath

as she approached him. His chest rose and fell, with shallow breaths. His skin was pale and clammy.

The gnome joined her and scanned the sky. "We need to move. We are only half way to the portal."

A howl erupted from the forest.

The colour drained from her face. "How did the creature get here so fast?"

He brandished his axe, and stepped between her and the forest. "It must have been waiting for us."

"But it was just at the cottage."

"It was not at the cottage," he replied.

Sally eyes wide. "What did you do?"

He flung out his arm in the direction of the forest. Trees cracked in the distance, echoing in the other direction. The howl thundered towards it.

"That will not distract it for long."

"Red?" Sally didn't move.

He shifted uneasily.

"The flapping wings chasing us at the cottage? The creature wasn't at the cottage, was it?" She narrowed her eyelids. Lightning flashed in the clouds gathering above them. "You manipulated me."

"And I would do it again," he said, "to save you and your aunt's friend."

Trees shuddered in the distance.

"We need to get him on his feet." He grabbed Alfred's arm. "You can scold me later. Right now, you need to heal your friend."

"I ca—"

"You can, and you will."

"I can't use *Wild Magick*." The air chilled. "It can't

be controlled. What if I—" She wasn't in the hospital with machines and science to rely on now. There she was confident; she knew the rules, but with magic, she was still a novice. Her voice broke. "It's dangerous."

He grasped her arm. "I—. We didn't spend the last four days traipsing through this world to have you buckle at the crucial moment."

Lighting exploded above them. It flicked along Sally's injured forearm. The smell of ozone wrapped around her. Sparks flared at the ends of her fingers.

Dark red clouds, edged with slivers of bright pink, hovered above them, casting shadows on the ground.

An almighty roar rumbled over the forest. The trees convulsed.

"It is coming. We need to get him out of here," he said.

"I don't know how," said Sally.

"How did we get here?" he asked.

"I didn't…" Her hands trembled. "I don't know."

A low whisper caught on the wind. It grew louder and multiplied.

Sally's heart raced.

The smell of gingerbread flooded over her. An army of garden gnomes swarmed over her, morphing into gingerbread fae as they scratched, and wiggled, and squeezed into her mouth. Their weight crushed her chest.

She gasped for air, and clawed at her skin, trying to free herself.

Their colours faded; shadows now flicked over her skin.

Red's calm voice rose above the clamour. "What did you do?

"I— I panicked!" She curled her arms and legs to her

chest.

"And are you panicking now?" he asked.

"Too bloody right!"

"Look at your hands." He instructed.

Sally stared at her fingers. Her fingertips burned bright orange. Sparks licked along her fingers, pricking the skin where they touched.

"You must control it." He glanced back towards the forest. "Focus."

Her fingertips changed colour, shifting from orange, to blue, then silvery-white, the pricking less painful, now.

Red touched her arm and spoke in a gentle voice: "You can do this."

Sally nodded. She had no choice. She crouched next to Alfred.

Her hands trembled as she placed them on Alfred's chest.

Red rose slowly. "But you need to do it quickly."

She took a deep breath, feeling the current of energy flow through her. The metal plate buzzed in her right forearm.

She slipped one arm under Alfred's head, removed her injured arm from the sling, and placed it on his chest.

Sally focused on the energy surrounding her, flowing over her skin, and through her veins. She concentrated on Alfred, and whispered. "*Sana.*"

The sparks faltered and fizzled at the ends of her fingers.

"I told you, I *can't.*" She slumped onto her knees.

"That is just your fear." Red continued to scan the sky. "Forget your Protector training. Just let the *Wild Magick* flow through you. Give in to it. See what you want to happen," he whispered. "I will not tell anyone."

Sally knelt forward, unbuttoned Alfred's shirt, and placed

her hands back on his chest, and took another - very - deep breath to centre herself.

Heat washed over her body. Not painful this time, but warm and comforting. She closed her eyes and drew on her medical knowledge, replaying the procedure in her mind:

One: elevate the wound above the heart. Done.

Two: increase fluids. Problematic, but doable once they were safe.

Three: keep patient immobilised, and allow to sleep. There was no time for that, right now.

A drop of rain fell onto her cheek.

Her heart skipped. She concentrated on the storm clouds. Rain trickled down her arm, sizzled along the heated metal plate in her forearm, and through her fingertips, soaking into Alfred's skin.

Alfred stirred, but remained unconscious. She delved deeper, searching his body for any injuries or - her blood ran cold - or damage to the brain.

He twitched.

Sally held her breath and prodded further. Still nothing.

The colour returned to his cheeks.

She let out a slow, ragged breath.

He opened his eyes.

"It's a trap," he hissed. "It needs you to get through the portal."

"Death on a—" Red shifted his weight.

Sally jumped to her feet. Sparks still spat from her fingertips. She heard it too: a howling roar, trees splitting and crashing to the ground.

"You need to hurry."

Another almighty roar erupted from the forest.

"We need to leave. Now!" Red grabbed Alfred's arm as he dashed past him, and half-dragged him towards the portal.

Sally stumbled after them, drawing on the energy around her for one last effort. She sprinted through the waist-high grass after them.

"I see what you did there." she yelled at Red.

"Who me?" Red yelled back.

"I hate you." She smiled and ran faster.

"I know." He grinned. "Tell me about it later."

An explosion of splintering, crashing, and roaring burst from the forest. Shattered trees jettisoned skyward. Heavy footsteps reverberated through the ground.

Sally glanced over her shoulder. A massive shadow shot up into the sky. Debris crashed back into the trees. The shadow hovered, then - with an ear-piercing wail, cleared the trees and darted towards the ground. Each flap of its huge wings flattened the grass as it skimmed just above the glade towards them.

"Run, Sally!" Red's frantic voice almost drowned out by the portal's groans.

He paused in front of the portal and propped Alfred up.

She still had a hundred metres before she reached them.

A burst of energy erupted inside her, drawing *magick* out of her as it had done, when she'd healed Alfred. But this time, it wouldn't let go. Sally strained to sever the connection. The *Wild Magick* twisted deeper, tearing at her gut.

She kept running.

Tears streamed down her face. She remembered Agnes, still recovering, almost a year later, from *Wild Magick* wielded by The Collector working for The Dark.

Her body shuddered.

She stumbled.

Shit! All magick had a price.

Sally slowed, shuffling as her energy dwindled.

The winged shadow creature was almost upon her.

Shit.

Its icy breath chilled her to the bone.

Shit, shit, shit.

Her hand spasmed. Her fingers crackled, and her skin burned. Light flashed into the air, slamming into the creature.

The air rippled and shimmered.

The creature flinched. Its outline flickered. Waves of shimmering blue washed over it, revealing a huge iridescent creature with scales as large as her head, shifting through a kaleidoscope of colours, caught in a net of light. Unable to move. Its long, serpentine neck flailed. Leathery wings tipped with claws beat furiously against their magical bonds.

A flare of searing light, and the creature was blasted back, towards the forest. The blue light collapsed, and the creature was invisible, a creature of smoke once more carving a scar through the glade.

Sally's connection to the *Wild Magick* snapped. The clouds vanished. She recoiled towards the portal.

She doubled over, trying to catch her breath. Her heart thumped. Her knees threatened to buckle.

"Sally," Red yelled over the roar of the portal's wind.

She raised her head.

He shoved Alfred into the portal and pointed over her shoulder.

"Now what?" Her shoulders slumped.

The grass was shifting. The shadow was moving.

"Oh, hell." She shuffled towards the portal, almost falling

as she reached him.

The creature shrieked. Behind her, wings faltered and footsteps stomped.

"Death's head on a mopstick!" she cursed. "Dragons are real?" she squeaked as launched herself towards the portal.

"I saw." He grabbed her hand and swung her into the swirling light of the portal. His lips moved but his voice was swallowed up by its ravenous groan.

White light flashed in the corner of Sally's eye as she entered.

To Sally, portals were simply pain. Pain slicing in her gut, a thousand metal-tipped claws scrabbling in her brain, nightmarish hallucinations, and shrill screams piercing her ears and pounding in her head. Wings thrashed in the darkness. And a deep, grinding pain twisted in the bone of her right forearm.

But, this time, it wasn't animated garden gnomes that taunted her, instead the over-powering stench of ginger smothered her. Gingerbread fae bombarded her, like a swarm of giant, insatiable mosquitoes intent on devouring her flesh, nibbling, biting, and cramming themselves into her mouth. They crumbled over her face and rammed in her nostrils, suffocating her.

And, in the darkness, a ghostly, winged shadow loomed.

Waiting…

chapter thirteen

The jingle of bells faded. A jolly laugh echoed in Sally's ears. Ho, ho, ho. The music got louder.

A wall of hot air slammed into her.

Sally was thrown onto the ground and landed on a patch of dry, spiky grass. There was a dull thud beside her.

Her arm shuddered under her weight. She rolled onto her back.

Sunlight streamed into her eyes. A flash of white flickered in the corner of her eye.

She threw her arm over her eyes. The sling pulled taut on the back of her neck. The bones ground in her forearm. She swallowed down the nausea, and peered at the sky. The sun was low in the sky; it was late.

She sighed with relief. Only one sun; she was home. That was a good start.

A faint smell of grass fire smoke hung in the air. A Christmas carol warbled inside her aunt's cottage. Alfred's shredded suit jacket lay crumpled beside her.

Sally strained to prop herself up on her injured arm.

Beads of sweat dripped down her forehead. The borrowed attire may have protected her from the Otherworld's chill but, here in the sweltering heat, it proved a liability. She wriggled the arm half way out of the sleeve of the thick woollen coat.

The portal belched behind her.

"Sally!" Agnes' voice was close.

Sally wiped the sweat from her eyes and blinked to clear her vision.

"Thank the Gods you're back." Agnes tucked back a curl of snow-white hair behind one ear. "The portal has been collapsing for over an hour."

She took Sally's left hand and helped her to her feet.

"How long were we gone?" Sally let the woollen coat fall to the ground.

"You're back in time for Christmas dinner." Agnes ran her fingers along the collar of the linen shirt Sally was wearing. "This is a new look for you." She shook her head. "You must be broiling. Let's get you out of these clothes."

Aunt Enid wobbled and lowered her silver cane. The glowing lines of Aether tracing the carvings along its length faded.

The portal's light flickered fitfully over them.

Enid leaned on her cane. Worry lines edged her eyes. Her skin was pale grey. She looked old; older than Sally had ever seen her.

Alfred moaned beside them.

"Alfred!" Enid lurched to his side, slid down her cane onto her knees, and embraced him.

Sally gritted her teeth and braced her arm tight to her chest.

Alfred's trousers were torn at the knees, his shoes caked with mud and his windswept hair stood up in every direction like he'd been electrocuted.

"You look terrible," she said.

"You don't look so crash hot yourself," he replied.

A dark charcoal blur darted across the back yard, trailing a strand of silver tinsel behind it. Sally crouched down to receive the incoming feline.

Mr B rushed past her and curled around Alfred's legs.

Sally frowned and rose slowly.

Alfred leaned down and removed the tinsel. Mr B arched his back.

Enid raised an eyebrow. "Looks like you've made a new friend."

Alfred smiled

"We have an understanding." He scratched Mr B behind the ears. "Yes?"

Mr B purred and rubbed his chin against Alfred's tattered trouser leg.

Alfred chuckled.

"Let me take a look at your arm." Agnes removed the sling and rolled Sally's arm over.

Sally flinched. Tears welled up in her eyes.

"That's not good." Agnes cradled Sally's arm, closed her eyes, and recited the healing word: "*Sana.*"

Her hands trembled.

Sally's arm buzzed briefly. Then nothing.

Agnes' shoulders slumped.

"Powers still on the fritz?" Alfred dusted off his trousers.

"I'm conserving my energy." Agnes pursed her lips tightly. Dark circles were visible under her eyes.

"Please let me." Enid cradled Sally's arm and felt the bone. "Oh, dear. Is that the arm you broke at my… as a child?"

Sally nodded.

"I didn't know you had an implant," said Agnes.

"I'd forgotten about it until—" She eyed Enid. She was still angry at her aunt using *Memory Magic* to change her memories of the incident, without permission. But now, as an adult, she could understand; magic, Protectors, and Otherworlds, were probably too much for a ten-year-old to comprehend.

"Ah, yes." Enid smiled uneasily. "I am sorry," she whispered. She placed a hand on either side of Sally's forearm and closed her eyes. "*Sana.*"

Warmth bathed Sally's skin and radiated along it. Then stopped. Her arm twinged.

Sally slowly extended her arm. A sharp pain radiated along her arm. She winced and snapped it back to her chest. The bone throbbed.

"Hmmm." Enid frowned. "That's odd."

Agnes peeked over Enid's shoulder. "Perhaps being in an Otherworld has affected how our magic is working on her."

Or Wild Magick? Sally swallowed. What was the punishment for using forbidden *magick*?

"I've lost my cufflinks." Alfred frowned and straightened his shirt cuffs. "And I seem to have misplaced my waistcoat."

Sally answered, glad to have a change in subject. "I'm afraid it's stuffed in a bin on the other side of the portal." She picked up his damaged coat. "Your jacket made it back." She shook off the grass. "Though it is worse for wear."

She handed it to him.

Alfred wiped his hand over his jacket.

His fingers caught in the long tears in the fabric.

"Damn. That was my sleuthing suit." He inspected the torn red silk lining. "It was my favourite."

"We'll get you a new one." Enid patted his arm.

The Christmas music, wafting from the cottage played another joyful chorus.

Alfred scanned the yard near the portal. "Where's Red?"

At Sally's feet, where Alfred's jacket had been deposited, was a ceramic garden gnome, toppled head-first into a tuft of grass.

"I almost forgot." Agnes pulled a silver and sapphire amulet from her pocket. She pressed it into Sally's hand and closed her hand over it.

It hummed in Sally's hand; the Aether pricked her skin. It felt somehow different from what she remembered. Less connected. She swallowed; did it know she'd used *Wild Magick*? Did amulets get jealous?

She hesitated, forced a smile, and slipped it around her neck. It felt cool against her skin.

The Christmas music faded. A single bell heralded the next song. A shiver ran down her spine. She glanced around to list five things that she could…

A wave of exhaustion swept over her. She'd only made it this far on pure adrenalin, and her reserves were dwindling. The *Wild Magick* had left her feeling like she'd been through her aunt's old clothes ringer.

A lone bee buzzed near her head. She waved it away and pressed the ball of her hand against her forehead.

"Let's get you inside. A cup of tea is what you both need." Aunt Enid slipped her arm around Alfred's and ushered him inside the cottage.

Mr B extricated himself from Alfred's ankles and ran ahead of them.

"Just a minute." Sally leaned over and picked up Red.

His dark, pupil-less eyes stared back. His axe was firmly held in one hand, the other now missing the glove left behind in the forest. A hint of armour glinted under his scarlet coat.

She'd agreed to talk about her searching through his things when they'd returned home, yet he knew he'd be silenced. She wiped specks of dirt and grass off his cap.

"I'm sorry," she whispered.

Static drifted along the hallway of her aunt's cottage as Sally approached the back door.

She placed Red on the back verandah. The screen door slammed shut behind her.

In the lounge room, the needle scratched on her aunt's old record turntable. A Christmas carol started playing, slowly, eerily, then stuck on one note; the ring of a sleigh bell repeating over and over.

Sally's muscles tensed. Her fingers tingled. She curled them tight against her palm, took a deep breath, then stretched them. She was in control.

She entered the lounge room, removed the needle from the record, and replaced it in its cradle.

Sally had changed into a light cotton sundress; she was relieved to be out of the heavy clothes and leather boots she'd found at the cottage. She wiggled her toes and cooled herself under the air conditioner, relieved it hadn't broken down this summer.

She shifted in the armchair by the lounge window. Her shoulder brushed against the adorned pine tree wedged behind it. A faint scent of stale pine descended on her. Above her, a silver bauble shivered precariously as a branch scraped the ceiling.

Alfred draped the silver tinsel on the tree and sat on the settee, opposite the air conditioner, leaving the cat's favourite armchair empty.

China cups clinked in the kitchen.

"How about some gingerbread men?" Aunt Enid's voice carried across the hallway.

Agnes popped her head through the lounge room door. "They're fresh out of the oven. She's been stress-baking again."

Alfred's fingers tightened on the arm of the settee.

Sally's stomach churned. The nightmares she'd had each night in the Otherworld still haunted her; gingerbread was the last thing she wanted at the moment.

She grimaced. They both looked at each other, their faces mirroring their shared apprehension.

"No, thank you," she replied.

Alfred swallowed. "Do you have any scones?" he asked loudly. "And some of your delicious lemon butter?"

Enid's reply wafted back: "Do I have scones?" She chuckled.

"There's a batch just gone in the freezer. I'll fetch them." Agnes paused at the doorway and winked. "She's made two batches while you were gone." She trotted along the hall.

The back door fly screen slapped shut.

Alfred puffed out his cheeks, and pulled at the neckline

of his crocheted cotton waistcoat adorned with a reindeer head, strewn with holly, and circled with sleigh bells.

"Nice waistcoat," Sally smiled. "Is that your new 'sleuthing suit'?"

He straightened it. "Your Great Aunt crocheted it for me, especially for Christmas."

Agnes arrived with a plate of sliced fruitcake covered in a generous layer of white icing.

"Enid's already sneaked a slice," she said. "She'll never admit it, but she did say it was better than her own." She offered some to Alfred.

His hand hovered over the cake for a second. His shoulders trembled.

"Actually, I think I'd prefer a scone," he said.

Agnes raised an eyebrow.

"They should be ready by now." She placed the plate on the coffee table and scuttled out the door.

A tingle ran down Sally's right arm as she reached for a slice. She stretched out her arm and flexed her fingers, then turned her arm over to examine it. Pain still clawed at the bone.

"Still bothering you?" asked Alfred.

"It's taking a long time to heal properly," Sally replied. "Maybe it's a lingering effect of the," she lowered her voice, "*Wild Magick*?"

Agnes returned with a plate of lemon-buttered scones.

"Pardon?" She glanced over her shoulder towards the kitchen, where Enid was cursing at the coffee maker. She thumped its base. It spat at her, then finally settled into a rhythmic gurgle.

Agnes leaned in closer as she placed the plate of scones

on the coffee table next to the fruitcake. "Did you say: *Wild Magick*?"

Mr B rubbed against Alfred's legs, and curled his tail around his calves as he circled, then jumped up onto the coffee table and lay down in a shaft of late afternoon sun. He eyed Sally with a single, open eye.

"I had no choice," replied Sally. "Alfred was… sick. And I didn't… I couldn't… Red said…" She swallowed. "I had no choice."

She fidgeted with the amulet at her neck, tracing the edges of the sapphire amulet. It chilled in her palm. Something was off; it hadn't felt right since she returned. Perhaps the *Wild Magick* still lingered within her?

"Let's not mention it to Enid, eh?" whispered Agnes.

"I have no idea what you're talking about." Alfred picked up a scone slathered with a large dollop of lemon butter, and licked his lips. "But I won't tell."

"But she used it last year," Sally replied.

"And she's been out of sorts ever since," replied Agnes. "She exhausted herself keeping the portal open 'til you returned.

Sally tugged at the plastic bracelet around her wrist and nodded. She felt like a part of herself was missing. The feeling of raw *magick* still surged through her body. It felt different to channelling the Aether via an amulet; it was intoxicating - once she'd accepted it.

She closed her eyes and drew in a long, slow breath. *And dangerous.*

"Sally?" Agnes' voice pulled her back to this world's reality, where words shaped the Aether and magic was safe. Predictable. Structured.

"Hmmm?" She scanned the bookshelf under the window, next to her.

A pocket-sized Latin phrase book was wedged between a crochet pattern book and a treatise on bee keeping.

"Are you all right?" asked Agnes.

Sally snapped her palm over to cover the bracelet around her wrist.

"I will be," she replied. "I'm just tired." She pulled out the phrase book and flipped through its pages. "I really should brush up on my Latin."

Agnes smiled.

Cups rattled against a jar of honey as Aunt Enid laid a tray on the coffee table next to Mr B. Amber light spilled from the jar as it caught the sun.

Agnes sat in the empty armchair next to Sally. "Time to open presents."

Enid placed a tea cup - cream with a pink rose design - in front of Alfred.

"I'm glad my two boys are finally getting along." She scratched Mr B's ear. "You know you're not supposed to sit on the table, Mr B."

She sat on the settee next to Alfred and patted his hand.

The cat's tail twitched. He rose slowly, stretched, and stepped off the table, reaching a paw across to Alfred, and oozed onto his lap.

"We've come to an agreement." He bit into the scone.

Mr B kneaded his lap.

"Since you got home?" She poured a cup of tea for him, then one each for Sally and Agnes.

"Ah, before," he sipped the tea, "because of the portal, you could say."

"Because of the portal?" asked Agnes.

"It's a long story," he replied.

Enid drizzled honey into her coffee. "We've got time."

Alfred leaned back into the settee and stroked the cat's dark charcoal fur.

"It all began when I came out to fix Sally's car radio…"

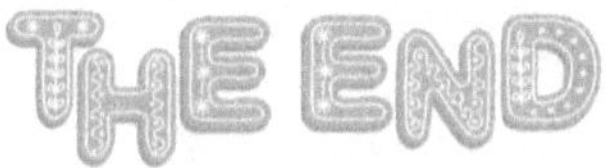

about this book

For my readers of *The Aunt Enid Mysteries*, please note this isn't your usual mystery, with hidden magic and mysteries set in Adelaide, in our world.

Twixtmas is a portal fantasy, set in one of the many Otherworlds occasionally accessible from our world via naturally occurring Thin Places, or portals created by magic.

about magic vs magick

The Protectors form 'magic' using words to shape Aether, channelled through them via a Focus. This form of magic is most common on our world, and is easier to learn and control.
Wild Magick is channelled directly by the user - usually born with innate abilities, and with an affinity for a specific form of *Wild Magick*. It is drawn directly from the energy that surrounds us, and is often unpredictable for the unexperienced or those not powerful enough to shape it.

Wild Magick hasn't been used knowingly for millenia, and its use is forbidden to The Protectors.

All *magick* has a cost.

acknowledgements

Thank you to David Carlisle and Sharon Kemmett; without their help and expertise, this book would still be a work in progress.
Thank you to my Patrons and readers for their support, and patience during the last year.

My thanks, also, to Cassandra Adams (who makes the most amazing gingerbread), for her advice on available, modern substitutes to update the recipe for Sunderland Nut biscuits (gingerbread biscuits) found in the 1861 edition of Mrs Beeton's *The Book of Household Management*.

Finally, thank you to David Brooks, whom I first met when he was the local historian for the Tea Tree Gully Library, (and now works for the The State Library of South Australia. You should check out the historic Mortlock Wing, which has inspired a few of my stories and may be featured in a future Aunt Enid story), for introducing me to the reports and stories of sightings in the Tea Tree Gully area and Adelaide Hills of the local thylacine, nicknamed The Howler.

The Howler has featured in previous *Aunt Enid* books, and a short story written for the 2016 Adelaide Fringe exhibition '*A Trail of Tales*', supported by the Tea Tree Gully Library.

about the author

Karen J Carlisle lives in Adelaide with her family and the ghost of her ancient Devon Rex cat. She loves fantasy fiction, gardening, historical re-creation, and steampunk and can often be found plotting fantastical, piratic or airship adventures. Karen has always loved chocolate and rarely refuses a cup of tea. She is not keen on South Australian summers.

www.karenjcarlisle.com

You can support Karen at:
www.patreon.com/KarenJCarlisle
ko-fi.com/karenjcarlisle

Follow Karen at:
www.tiktok.com/@karenjcarlisle
www.youtube.com/@Karen-J-Carlisle
bsky.app/profile/karen-j.bsky.social
substack.com/@karenjcarlisle
www.instagram.com/karenjcarlisle
www.facebook.com/KarenJCarlisle

Where to buy Karen's books:
books2read.com/ap/nmAy7z/Karen-J-Carlisle

Leave a review at:
app.thestorygraph.com/profile/karenjcarlisle
www.goodreads.com/KarenJCarlisle

Sign up for Karen's newsletter:
karenjcarlisle.com/sign-up-email-list/

o t h e r   w o r k s   b y   k a r e n   j   c a r l i s l e

Available in paperback and eBook:
The Adventures of Viola Stewart series:
Doctor Jack & Other Tales: Journal #1
Eye of the Beholder & Other Tales: Journal #2
The Illusioneer & Other Tales: Journal #3
Tomorrow, When I Die: A Christmas Story

James Findlay Journals
Blood Ties

The Aunt Enid Mysteries
Aunt Enid: Protector Extraordinaire
A Fey Tale
Twixtmas: An Aunt Enid Christmas Story (of sorts)

The Department of Curiosities
The Department of Curiosities

Available as eBooks:
Short Story Collections
With a Twist of the Nib: For when time is short
Another Twist of the Nib: Shorter Tales with a Darker Twist
Quarantine Reads: Escape to Adventure
Cogs and Conspiracies: A collection of steampunk short stories

Mrs Hudson Investigates
Mrs Hudson Investigates
The Case of the Forgotten Letter

Coming soon
Against the Empire (Department of Curiosities 2)

bonus extras

aunt enid's gingerbread recipe

(based on mrs beeton's 1861 recipe)

Aunt Enid would've read this very book, and baked the original recipe herself. (If you want to know the SPOILERS, then read books one and two.) Her recipe is based on Mrs Beeton's own Sunderland nut biscuit recipe. It must've been a huge hit, as her recipe calls for quantities of ingredients large enough to feed a small army (or a hungry extended family).

I've sized down the quantities and converted to metric (this means a UK/Australian cup measure, ie. 250ml), and adapted the recipe to ingredients more readily available to modern-day cooks. The original recipe called for treacle. I substituted golden syrup.

Thank you to Cassandra Adams, who makes delicious gingerbread. She wouldn't share her secret recipe, but gave me advice on substitutes for mine.

aunt enid s gingerbread recipe

Adapted by Karen Carlisle.

Ingredients:
200g golden syrup
1/2 cup brown sugar
1/2 cup (114g) butter or margarine (I'm lactose intolerant)
2 1/3 cup plain flour (312g)
2 tablespoon ginger
2 tablespoon allspice

Method:
Add flour, sugar, ginger, and allspice to a bowl and mix well.

Warm golden syrup and butter together. (You can warm in microwave in short bursts, until butter has softened and mixes, checking every 10 seconds, so not to overheat.)

Work liquids into flour, with a spoon, until consistency of smooth paste. Cover mixture with cling wrap and leave to sit in fridge for a couple of hours.*

Roll mixture on tray covered with baking paper, to approx. 1/2cm thickness.

Bake in oven at approx. 140°C for 25-30 minutes, depending on your oven. Note: biscuits are soft when first out of oven. They will harden as they cool.

Makes 20-25 biscuits, depending on size and shape of cutter.
Time: 20-30 minutes, plus 20-30 cooking time.

*(This is supposed to make the mixture easier to work with, but I skipped this because I'm a 'lazy cook'. The biscuits still turned out delicious and chewy, just how I like my gingerbread. If the mixture becomes too soft to handle, put in fridge for a while.)